LISA MILLER HUGHES—to save her son's good name, she enters into a marriage that is a farce from the outset.

TOM HUGHES—unable to leave the killing behind in Vietnam, he now faces charges of murder at home.

LIZ TALBOT STEWART—while she nurses her dying husband, she fights to hold onto the man she loves.

DAN STEWART—free at last to marry the woman he has always loved, he finds that happiness is cruelly fleeting.

———————————

Series Story Editor **Mary Ann Cooper** is America's foremost soap opera expert. She writes the nationally syndicated column *Speaking of Soaps*, is a major contributor to leading soap opera magazines, and is a radio and television personality.

John Boyd, who wrote *Horizons of the Heart*, lives in Larchmont, New York. In his spare time, he plays the violin and writes music.

Dear Friend,

In 1963, the country was rocked by news of the assassination of President John F. Kennedy. Many Americans learned of the tragedy when their favorite soap opera, AS THE WORLD TURNS, was interrupted by a special report. Over the years, fans of AS THE WORLD TURNS have used the serial as a reference point to events in the news and in their lives. Many fans can remember Tom Hughes as a little boy as vividly as they remember their own children. If soaps mirror life, is it any wonder that we get so involved in them?

Book 4 of our *Soaps & Serials* series, *Horizons of the Heart*, tugs at our heartstrings as we watch the Hughes family work through a life and death crisis. One can't help but admire their determination and courage. Oakdale's stalwart family has remained intact to this day for just this very reason.

For Soaps & Serials Books,

Mary Ann Cooper

Mary Ann Cooper

P.S. If you missed our previous novelizations of AS THE WORLD TURNS and can't find them in your local book source, see the order form inserted in the back of this book.

AS THE WORLD TURNS

4

Horizons of the Heart

PIONEER COMMUNICATIONS NETWORK, INC.

Horizons of the Heart

AS THE WORLD TURNS paperback novels are published and distributed by Pioneer Communications Network, Inc.

SOAPS & SERIALS™ is a trademark of Pioneer Communications Network, Inc.

ISBN: 0-916217-44-2

Printed in the United States of America

10 9 8 7 6 5 4 3 2 1

Horizons of the Heart

Chapter One
A Time of Tension

Oakdale 1969

Paul Stewart could remember when Saturday had been one of his favorite days. He paused a moment and looked up from the report he was studying. Those first months of marriage with his beautiful English-born Liz had been good ones, or at least they had seemed so. Those leisurely Saturday morning breakfasts—usually their baby Betsy napped while Liz and he shared the toasted scones she always insisted on and made their plans for the weekend. Their differences were so few then and so easily solved. She brewed her tea and he made his coffee.

God, how he loved her! Even now he loved her, as he sacrificed his Saturday golf and slaved at the office to bring in more money to meet the demands for what he considered luxuries, for what she termed necessities. He returned to his report, and the figures seemed to squirm before his eyes. At the first throbbing pain of another of those damn headaches he brought his hand to his forehead in a soothing gesture.

All this extra work was obviously straining his eyes. Briefly he closed them, and competing with the dull ache in his head was the lovely vision of Liz with Betsy in her arms. Her baby, it was true, but now Betsy was his baby too. The adoption had gone through quickly. The true father, his adopted brother Dan, had raised no objections. The pain in his head increased almost on signal at the thought of Dan. Liz had sworn she would forget him forever. But had she? Would she?

The telephone rang.

"Paul!" It was Liz, her English accent strident and somehow accusing.

"What's the matter, honey?"

"Our air conditioner has broken down—*that's* the matter." In the background he could hear Betsy crying. "It's stifling in here," she continued. "Oh, how I hate these Illinois summers!" Her voice rose in hysteria.

"Easy, honey," he said. "I'll call the repair people. And then I'll come home. We'll drive out to the lake this evening. Maybe a picnic—"

She broke in. "Make the call, Paul."

Another expense, he thought, as he replaced the receiver. It wasn't her fault, but would these mounting bills never stop?

The picnic wasn't a success, and it should have been. Ellen, Paul's stepmother, and David Stewart, his father, had eagerly agreed to take care of Betsy for a couple of hours. At Danny's Delicatessen, Paul had ordered roast beef sandwiches and Danny's special potato salad, both of which Liz loved. For a secret surprise he had stopped by Mrs. Clarke's Tea Shoppe and bought two servings of English trifle for their dessert. Now that they sat at a lakeside picnic table, they scarcely touched the food before them. There was a lake breeze, cool and refreshing. White clouds floated overhead tinged with the scarlet of the sunset, and the lake reflected the same scarlet.

"Red sky at night, sailor's delight," Paul said.

Liz, ignoring his comment, stared out over the lake, lost in a private world of her own. Finally, she turned to Paul. "We must have a nursemaid for Betsy," she said firmly. "I'll call an agency Monday."

"Liz!" Paul's voice was harsh with desperation. "We can't afford a nursemaid. We simply have to cut costs, not add to them."

She began crying.

"I'm sorry, honey," Paul continued more gently, "but can't you understand? There's more outgo than income." The headache was coming back, but he went on, pressing his forehead hard with his hand as if he could push back the pain. "Maybe you should get rid of the bookstore," he said quietly. "It's losing money."

Liz broke in quickly. "That's just it. When I bought Wade's Bookstore and managed it personally, it made money. The woman I put in charge just before Betsy was born has let things slide. Oh, Paul, can't you see? With a nursemaid for Betsy I could be at the bookstore every day and make it pay. We'd have more money. We could be happy!"

On the way home both were silent. Paul was thinking, *I mustn't be selfish. Of course, I want Liz home, but it must be confining for her.* And maybe she would make the bookstore work again. Or would it be just another gamble that didn't pay off? Why was he so confused, so suddenly tired? He couldn't think straight anymore. . . .

Liz's head teemed with plans for the bookstore. She

would be in charge again. Immediately the bookstore would be closed for minor redecorating, a couple of weeks at the most. It wouldn't cost much and it would be money well invested. Then there would be the grand reopening, Liz greeting old and new customers. A tea, perhaps, with Liz pouring, dressed simply. Understated elegance. She would select a new dress with care. Her eyes were shining. Bills would be paid promptly. Success would bring love to their marriage. They would live happily ever after, just the way it was in the many novels she would sell. Impulsively she squeezed Paul's arm.

When they pulled up in front of the elder Stewarts' house, they saw, in the driveway, the sleek new Buick convertible that they both recognized as Dan's. It was an awkward situation that they'd have to handle carefully. "Do you want to wait in the car while I pick up Betsy?" Liz asked. Already Paul was getting out of the car by way of an answer.

Dan was nowhere to be seen when they entered the living room. "Betsy's asleep," Ellen Stewart informed them. "I'll get her."

David Stewart stood behind his wife. "Betsy's a doll," he said. "What a privilege to have her here even for a couple of hours." Ellen started to leave the room.

"Wait, just a minute," Liz said. "I want you to hear about our plans." Her face looked more alive, happier, than Paul could ever remember.

"First we're going to get a live-in nursemaid," Liz told them. "And then I'm going back to the bookstore full time, and really make a go of it."

Live-in nursemaid, Paul repeated to himself. Bookstore full time. She was off and running, all right.

"I'll close Wade's a couple of weeks for some redecorating," Liz went on. "And then we'll have a reopening that will be the social event of Oakdale." As she whirled around with the delight of her own vision, Dan came into the room. For a moment he looked as though he might retreat, then he shrugged slightly and came forward.

"What's all this?" He turned in a slow imitation of Liz's pirouette.

Liz explained, and her enthusiasm was contagious. "Sounds great." Dan smiled. "Wade's wins again. Why don't you panel the storefront? Give Oakdale a little class."

Liz raised her hands in mock horror. "Too much mon-nee! I'll have to go slowly."

Dan looked at her seriously. "Would you consider an investor?"

Paul cleared his throat. When he spoke, his voice was cold and hard. "We'll manage this," he snapped.

Ellen Stewart hurried to the stairs. "I'll bring Betsy down now," she said.

When she returned with the sleeping child, the goodbyes were brief and hurried.

Liz lost no time. Early on Monday she called the agency and stated her needs. There was a pause, a rustling of papers, and then, "Could you come in this afternoon at three, Mrs. Stewart, and meet the person we think might be just right for you?" Liz could and did, after depositing Betsy once more with Ellen Stewart.

The agency office was cold, barren, and somewhat forbidding, but the warmth of the woman introduced to Liz soon overcame this. Her name was Nellie Owen, an ample woman with a bosom like a soft pillow and a face best described as honest and open. She was courteous but direct. "I'll need Sunday off, my church day, and one other half-day. Saturday afternoon would be convenient," she stated.

Paul could hurry home on Saturday afternoons, Liz thought. It would give him a chance to spend more time with Betsy.

The woman's references were excellent. She had been with the Carson family, whom Liz knew slightly, for the last ten years. The Carsons had left Oakdale. Mrs. Owen—Mr. Owen had passed away twelve years ago—could move in within the week. The salary was a bit more than Liz had had in mind. Still, seventy-five a week with room and board wasn't bad, and the agency lady assured Liz that she was getting a bargain. She hired Nellie Owen on the spot. It was only after she left the agency office that it occurred to her that she should have called Paul before making the decision.

The next two weeks were a whirl. First there was the visit to the Oakdale Bank. Paul met Liz there on the dot at eleven. He hated banks and he hated asking for the loan they would need to redecorate the bookstore and cover the expenses of expansion. Mr. Slide, the bank president, had piercing green eyes, the color of money, and a counterfeit smile. He listened carefully.

Paul admired Liz's organization. The figures she showed clearly indicated that the Wade's Bookstore profits had begun sliding the year she left and finally dipped slightly into the red. And her belief in herself was impressive. Her plans for putting Wade's in the black again were convincing.

From his heavy, solid, walnut chair, which to Paul seemed rather like a throne, Mr. Slide favored Liz with a smile that bordered on the benign. "I will need a little time to study these records," he said sonorously, "but I'm sure something can be arranged." He dismissed them with a smug, lordly graciousness.

The loan went through. The store was closed, and

the redecorating began. Liz was in her element. Wade's would become a browsing place as much as a buying place. There would be nooks where customers could sit and read the books they might buy. The big bay window that fronted the street would now have a roomy window seat for more browsers and buyers. Liz called Dan and sought his advice on the best paneling for the storefront, and there was time to find the correct outfit for the opening. She chose a long tweed skirt, perfect for her slim hips, and a no-nonsense, businesslike blouse, exquisite in its detail, with a perky bit of a bow tie for a whimsical touch. It was outrageously expensive, but absolutely right.

Meanwhile Mrs. Owen was proving a delight. Betsy adored her from the start, and without complaint Mrs. Owen added to her role of nursemaid the duties of housekeeper. Even Paul admitted that the household routine had never gone so smoothly, though the headaches persisted even when he didn't think of the increased expenses.

The opening of Wade's Bookstore was all Liz had hoped it would be. Oakdale turned out in full force.

"Liz, it's lovely and charming, and what's more, it makes me want to buy books." Ellen Stewart smiled over her teacup at Liz.

"And your silver tea service adds just the right touch," Liz responded. "Thanks for lending it to me."

Dan was at his mother's side. "It's the outside paneling that's bringing them in," he said. "Honestly, Liz, you've done wonders. I predict a business boom."

When Paul, who'd been detained at his office, arrived at almost six o'clock, he was amazed at how crowded the store still was. Liz greeted him with a tired smile. "Well, honey," he told her, "I don't know how much of a commercial success you have going, but you're a social success, that's for sure." His smile faded as he looked over the crowd and spotted Dan in earnest conversation with Chris, Bob and Nancy Hughes, old family friends. A book was in his hands and he appeared to be extolling its virtues. With a nod of his head Paul indicated to Liz that he had seen Dan. "One of your salesmen?" he queried sarcastically.

"Don't be a goose," Liz answered. "He came with Ellen and David to wish me well."

"I don't like his being here," Paul said in a low voice.

Liz' eyes flashed danger signals. "This is a bookstore open to the public, Paul, not a rendezvous." She smiled charmingly as Bob Hughes approached. "I wish I could offer you champagne, Bob," she said as she poured him a cup of tea.

Bob smiled. "This in itself is intoxicating, Liz." He surveyed the bookstore. "You've done yourself proud, and Oakdale too." He drifted away.

When Paul spoke to Liz again, his voice was controlled, almost gentle. "I'll stick around until you close the joint. Then we'll have a bite to eat. You must be exhausted."

Liz's smile was fixed and her voice, too, was controlled. "Be charming and mingle, dear." She rose and made her way slowly to stand by the door and thank the departing guests and remind them subtly that they were always welcome back as customers. As she said goodbyes, she observed Paul talking to Dan. The exchange was brief, their faces unsmiling. Then Dan turned, nodded to his parents, and strode toward the door. Liz's eyes searched the face that would always be dear to her, no matter what she promised or told herself. It was expressionless, no sign to betray what might have been said between Paul and him. Then she saw a careful smile and heard the genuine

14

warmth in his voice. "Congratulations, Liz."

She took his hand in hers. "Thank you, Dan, for all your help. Remember, if we don't have the latest books on medicine, we can order them. Service is our motto."

He paused as if to speak, then smiled, and left.

Ellen and David Stewart were the last to leave. "Paul and I are going out for a bite to eat as soon as I lock up," Liz told them. "Won't you join us?" Ellen and David glanced at Paul standing beside Liz. He said nothing.

"No, no," Ellen answered quickly, almost too brightly. "David has promised he'd buy me a hamburger and take me to see *True Grit*, but thank you."

As Paul and Liz drove to the restaurant, she turned to him. "That was rude, Paul."

"What was rude?"

"Not backing up my invitation to Ellen and David. You just stood there sulking."

"Look," Paul said, "let's not quarrel. You're tired, and I've had a rough day. Let's enjoy the peace and quiet of a good meal."

He drove on. He hadn't said where they were going and Liz didn't much care. It was true that she was tired, dog-tired, but she was also exhilarated. The mid-September air was hazy. Evening shadows crisscrossed the road, and the tall poplars on either side made a green tunnel, cool and relaxing. She sighed and half-dozed as they sped along.

"We're here," Paul announced. He had pulled up in front of a small, shingled building that looked almost like an English country inn. It was typical of Paul to try so hard to please her with all the props. The setting was perfect. It was the plot that never seemed to turn out right, no matter how hard he tried.

Their table in a corner was appropriately covered with a red checkered cloth, and there was the inevitable candle in a wax-encrusted green bottle. Paul ordered a bottle of wine. When it came, he offered a toast. "To you, Liz, and to Wade's. Every success!"

They made small talk, carefully avoiding any subject that might lead to a dispute. The steak was tender, thank heavens. The dessert was light and delicious. Paul ordered after-dinner drinks, though Liz was ready to head for home. Once again he toasted to their future. It was slightly irritating to Liz, as though he had little faith in their ability to make a go of things on their own, and he was calling on luck and the gods to see them through. The wine and then the brandy fanned her curiosity into a flame she could not control.

"What did you say to him?" she blurted out, almost against her will.

Paul said nothing.

"What did you say to Dan at my bookstore?" She waited.

Paul spoke evenly as though each word was measured carefully. "I told him I thought it was the best for all concerned if he stayed away from the store."

"How could you?" In her agitation she overturned the half-filled wine glass which hadn't been removed. Her just-right white blouse was splotched with an ugly red stain. She waved away the solicitous waiter while Paul hurriedly took care of the check.

As they drove home in angry silence, Paul massaged his forehead from time to time. That, Liz thought, was a habit that was becoming a bit irritating.

Chapter Two
The Green-Eyed Monster

In the weeks that followed the reopening of Wade's Bookstore, it was amazing how often Dan Stewart needed to order more medical books. Obviously he was paying no attention to Paul's suggestion that he stay away from the place, and just as obviously Liz was glad to see him. She teased him about his seeming lack of interest in any books outside the field of medicine. "Honestly, Dan, your reading is so one-sided, so professional. There's more to life than medicine." She talked him into buying some Samuel Beckett novels and plays. "He just won the Nobel Prize, you know."

When she learned that he had never heard of William Styron, she commanded him to buy and read *The Confessions of Nat Turner.* Dan enjoyed discussing with her the books she pressed on him. She was leading him into a new world, and he was seeing a new Liz, too—an intelligent, forceful woman of wide interests, a woman of depth and humor and concern for what was going on in the world, and in space as well. "Think of it," she said to Dan, "we've walked on the moon! What *can't* we do?"

"Neil Armstrong walked on the moon," he said. "You and I just look at it."

"I was with him," she retorted.

His visits to the bookstore became more frequent.

On a Friday afternoon in early November, Paul made a casual decision that precipitated many changes. A cold, relentless rain had been falling most of the day, and office matters were tied up for the weekend. Paul wasn't feeling up to par—maybe a cold was coming on—and decided to leave early. He would drive by the bookstore and pick up Liz. There wouldn't be much business on a dismal day like this. She could close up shop, or leave a clerk in charge. When he reached his car, he groaned. The right front tire was flat. For a moment, he was tempted to leave it there in the parking lot, go back to the office, and call a cab. It was not his nature to dodge responsibilities, however. Muttering harsh words at the car in general and the tire in particular, he changed it in the rain.

By the time he had finished the job, he was wet, out of sorts, and sorry for himself. He glanced at his watch. It was now only an hour before closing time at the bookstore. Surely Liz would be willing to leave. They could stop at the corner pub on the way home and have a drink while he dried out. It would put a little cheer into a cheerless day.

He parked on a side street around the corner from the bookstore. As he walked past the big bay window, he glanced in and suddenly stopped. There was Liz, and with her was Dan. They were laughing and, as he watched, Liz gave Dan a playful push and seemed to admonish him with a wagging finger in exaggerated schoolmarm style. Dan caught her hand and held it for just a moment, but to Paul they seemed to freeze in time. Breathing became difficult for him, and the all-too-familiar pain suddenly throbbed in his head. He paused in the pelting rain to gain some semblance of control and then quietly entered the bookstore.

They had the grace to look startled. There were no other customers. A clerk shelving books turned toward Paul as he closed the door behind him. He returned her greeting with a casual smile and a trite comment on the wet weather. It was as though there were two of him—an outside man acting a carefully rehearsed role and a man inside feeling his world fall apart.

It was Liz who spoke first. Looking at her watch, she asked, "Is there anything wrong?"

The inside man wanted to blurt out, *Yes, everything is wrong,* but the outside man simply said, "No. I just left the office early and came by to try and talk you into doing the same."

"Not a bad idea," Liz answered. She turned to the clerk. "You can go now." The girl gathered her things together preparing to leave.

"I'll be going too," Dan said.

"Not just yet," Paul said evenly. "We need to have a little talk."

Liz closed and locked the door after the departing clerk. She turned to the two men. "Let's not exaggerate this," she said.

"Is there something to exaggerate?" Paul asked. His voice was taut, almost at the breaking point.

"Look, Paul," Dan said, "I'm a customer. I buy books. We discuss them. It's no big deal."

Paul's words tumbled out. "As far back as I can remember, you've been a stinking problem to me, to everyone. And you've always tried to charm your way out of the troubles you've caused!"

Liz tried to interrupt, but Paul's harsh voice silenced her. "You've messed up Liz's life once, damn it! Are you trying again? You've got a wife. Leave my wife alone. And get out! Get out of here and get out of our lives."

Angry words were on the tip of Dan's tongue, but he looked at Liz and kept silent. Her eyes pleaded with him to leave. She unlocked the door and reluctantly he left in the rain.

"Let's go home," Paul said wearily as Liz turned away from the door.

"No, Paul, I—" The sentence was never finished; Liz watched as Paul, his face ashen, clutched at a bookshelf, and then fell to the floor.

In a matter of seconds, he had regained consciousness. Liz helped him up. "That was rather a melodramatic thing to do," she observed coolly.

Paul shook his head in disbelief. "I never fainted before in my life."

"How do you feel now?"

"Okay, I guess." But he seemed almost in a daze.

"I'll drive," Liz said.

They rode home without speaking. The rain beat a tattoo on the car roof. To Liz the windshield wipers seemed to say, Go away, go away, go away. From time to time, she glanced at Paul. He was staring straight ahead.

There were no drinks before dinner. Then after the meal, in which the silence was broken only by an occasional remark by Mrs. Owen as she clattered the dinner dishes, poured more tea for Liz, and replenished Paul's coffee, Liz went upstairs to spend time with Betsy. It was almost nine o'clock when she came into the study. Mrs. Owen had retired for the night. Paul was stretched out on the studio couch, his hand shading his eyes and concealing his mood.

"Are you asleep, Paul?"

He shook his head, but didn't remove his hand from his eyes.

"Listen to me, Paul."

He sat up.

"This isn't going to work. We can't go on like this." Her voice was low, nearly inaudible. "You're jealous of the bookshop. You're jealous of Dan. Sometimes I think you're even jealous of Betsy."

He started to protest.

"And you have a right to be. I promised I'd forget Dan, but I can't. Even when I'm in your arms, I think of him. You are just a substitute for the real thing. I'm happy only when I'm away from you, Paul. At the bookstore. With Dan. With Betsy. I've tried to love you, but all I feel is gratitude and guilt."

Paul waited for her to go on.

"We must get a divorce. This isn't a real marriage. It's like—it's like we're playing house. I'm the mommy. You're the daddy. And we're not even having a good time. The game is no fun."

The room seemed to spin before his eyes. Liz's voice became blurred, almost indistinct. *I'm not going to faint again*, Paul told himself, gripping the edge of the couch. He tried to concentrate on what Liz was saying as she continued her recital of their problems, his faults, and her unhappiness. The insidious headache which never seemed to leave entirely was growing in intensity. He held up his hand as if to stem her flow of complaints and was surprised to see that it was trembling. What was happening to him? He had never felt so out of control.

"Liz, Liz, Liz," he heard himself saying. He wanted to tell her how much he loved her. His love alone was enough for the two of them. It could surmount all her doubts and difficulties. "Liz, Liz, Liz," he repeated, as if just saying her name would bring her closer, into his arms.

She stopped talking.

"Give me a chance, honey. Give us a chance. I love you. I love Betsy. You're all I have—everything." The few words exhausted him. The pain was almost intolerable. The stairs leading to their bedroom seemed too steep to climb. He sank back on the couch. "Could you bring me my headache pills?" he asked.

She looked at him, not through the fog of her own self-concern, but really seeing him. His face was drawn, his brow wet with perspiration. "I'll help you to bed," she said.

He shook his head. "I'll just rest here for a while."

She left to get the pills. When she returned with the bottle and a glass of water, he smiled his thanks. "Not more than two," she told him, but he shook out four before she took the bottle away. "I'll get you a cover and a softer pillow." Moments later she was back, placing the pillow under his head, spreading the blanket over him. Her hand, cool and gentle, pressed against his forehead. He felt the sting of tears in his closed eyes.

"Would you like a cold cloth on your forehead?" she asked.

He shook his head. Now and then he would open his eyes slightly. She was there in a chair close by, idly turning the pages of a magazine. The pain was receding, and he was drifting, drifting away on a cloud. He wanted to reach out and hold on to her, but the cloud carried him farther away, and the sky darkened around him. He slept.

When he awoke, Liz was gone. For a moment, panic

gripped him. She had left him. And then he realized it must be quite late. She had merely gone upstairs to bed. In the dim light, he glanced at his watch. It was almost five o'clock. Pain still hovered in his head, but it was not as intense. He lay there reviewing the earlier scene. It was strange how little of the actuality he could recall. It seemed out of focus, a dream remembered indistinctly. Had it been that bad, really? Liz had been tired, overwrought. She couldn't have meant all the things she had said. They would patch things up. She would realize how much she and Betsy needed him.

And what about Dan? *Well,* he thought, *let's be fair. I've always resented Dan ever since Mom and Dad adopted him.* And he hated the custody fight over him—Dan the center of attention, Dan who'd seemed more important to his parents, David and Betty, than he himself had. When his mother had died, worn out by the long custody battle for Dan, Paul had blamed him for that in a way. Their life together had always been one of friction. Was it fair to think of Dan always as the problem-maker and of himself as the one who solved the problems?

It was late morning when he roused himself from a dreamless, almost numbing sleep. There was a note pinned to the blanket from Liz. She wrote that she was off to the bookstore battle.

It was a light, almost gay little note, as though the night before hadn't happened. He wondered if she too had had second thoughts.

Mrs. Owen hastily fixed him a light breakfast and left for her half-day off, and he devoted himself to Betsy-sitting. Life with a two-year-old, he reflected, was like living with a good-natured drunk. Betsy staggered about, falling down frequently, happily getting up again. She wasn't a demanding child, but her attention span was short. She didn't object when he put her in the playpen and sat close by reading. She played with toys and eventually curled up in a corner and went to sleep. At one o'clock he called Liz. Yes, he felt much better. Betsy was asleep. Mrs. Owen had dashed away for her mysterious Saturday rendezvous. He would start supper.

When Liz came home, it was nearly seven. He had fed Betsy, and she was playing a great banging-pans game in the kitchen while he peeled potatoes. Liz swooped her up for a welcome-home kiss. He hoped that she would give him one, too, but instead she carried Betsy away for her bath. By the time she was back from tucking Betsy into bed for the night, the simple meal of scrambled eggs, fried potatoes, and bacon was nearly ready.

Over the meal they made small talk. When they were stacking dishes in the dish washer, Liz stopped and turned to him. "How's your head tonight?"

"Same old head. Not an original thought in it."

"No, really."

"Well, doctor, there's a bit of a dull pain left over from last night, but that's all."

"Paul, you must see a doctor. Promise?"

It was a promise not hard to keep. On Sunday he was nearly incapacitated with a headache that even his tablets wouldn't dull. He spent the day in bed with the blinds drawn. Darkness seemed to blot out a bit of the pain. In the dim world of his consciousness, he was aware that Liz tiptoed in to check on him from time to time. Towards evening he felt somewhat better. She brought him milk toast on a tray. "I'll stay home in the morning and go with you to the doctor," she told him.

He didn't argue.

In the morning his head was better and he insisted that Liz go on to the bookstore as usual.

Dr. Morris's office was no different from most—impersonal, cheerless, with the requisite number of out-of-date, well-thumbed magazines. There were patients ahead of Paul, but no one he knew. They exchanged furtive, opaque looks, each wondering what affliction had brought the other to this place. The minutes crawled. At last a pretty nurse, who looked like a teenager, appeared in the doorway and announced to Paul that the doctor would see him now.

Dr. Morris was in his sixties, with a well-earned retirement not very far ahead. He had known Paul since he was a little boy. "Now, what's the matter, Paul?" he asked in much the same patronizing tone that he had used when Paul had broken his arm at the age of five.

Paul recounted his history of headaches, and along the way Dr. Morris asked probing questions as he pored over Paul's slim medical history which he was holding. There was the blood pressure bit, the stethoscope routine, and the penetrating light with which he searched Paul's eyes. "You should have some lab tests," he told Paul. "Could you go this afternoon?"

Paul nodded.

"And here's a prescription that should keep the pain in check. I'll call you toward the end of the week after I've had a chance to study the lab tests."

Paul thanked him and left.

It was a long week as he and Liz waited to hear from the doctor. Their relationship seemed to be on hold, as if both thought it best not to make the next move in their own lives until the doctor's verdict was in.

On Friday Dr. Morris called. "Well, Paul, how are you feeling? Is the medication helping those headaches?"

Paul assured him that he felt better.

"Just as a precaution, Paul, I want you to see a specialist. I've made an appointment for you. Got you in for ten o'clock tomorrow morning. Dr. Logan at Oakdale General. Okay?"

Paul wondered if he was imagining a note of urgency in Dr. Morris's voice.

. "Sure, I'll be there."

He was starting to dial Liz when the phone rang. It was his stepmother, Ellen. "Have you heard from Dr. Morris yet?" she asked. Paul said that there was no real news yet and that Dr. Morris was referring him to a specialist at Oakdale General, a Dr. Logan.

"We know him," Ellen said. "He's good. Your dad will be pleased that you're seeing him." Her voice was bright and cheerful.

Ellen was a loving person, Paul thought. She cared about people. And never, after she'd married his dad, had he detected any difference in her treatment of him and her own son Dan. She had devoted her time to them equally. He felt very close to her.

. He waited a bit and then phoned Liz. "Doc wants me to see a specialist at Oakdale tomorrow."

There was a brief silence. "Sounds like a good idea. See you soon, dear."

He hung up the receiver. She had called him "dear." So, as they waited, they were growing closer together. That was far more important to him than finding a cure for these stupid headaches. He felt better. They would have a pre-celebration.

He could hear Mrs. Owen bustling about in the kitchen. When she saw him in the doorway she said,

"Lunch is ready, Mr. Stewart. I've fixed a favorite of yours—pea soup. Do you a world of good."

She was a treasure. Liz had been right to hire her.

As she cleared the luncheon dishes, he remembered what he had meant to tell her. "Don't bother with an evening meal, Mrs. Owen. Liz and I will be going out for dinner tonight."

"How nice. You must be feeling better."

Paul smiled and nodded. He could hardly wait for Liz to get home as he visualized the evening ahead. Remembering the champagne he had stowed away for special occasions, he found a bottle and placed it in the refrigerator. He laid a fire in the fireplace. He made reservations at Oakdale's best restaurant. Before they went out to dinner, they would sit before the fire and drink a toast to the future.

Chapter Three
Best of Times, Worst of Times

"Here's to the best of times," Paul said.

Liz clink ' her glass against his. "I'll drink to that."

The burning logs in the fireplace filled the room with flickering shadows, giving it a comfortable, lived-in look.

Mrs. Owen stood in the doorway. "Betsy's asleep. Is there anything you'll be wanting before I go to my room?"

Liz shook her head, and Paul said, "Don't worry about the fireplace. I'll close the fire screen before we leave." They exchanged good nights.

The candles on the mantel added to the glow from the fire. It was pleasantly warm and cozy here. Paul put his arm around Liz and she snuggled against his shoulder. He regretted that he'd made the reservations, but he had, and now it was time to dress for their special outing.

The fire, the dancing shadows, were hypnotic. His lips brushed her hair. She raised her face to his. "Paul," she murmured, "I'm truly sorry for the stupid, hateful things I said. Try to forget them."

He smiled and kissed her, and she responded. Now she was encircled in his arms. She was his lovely Liz again. Like awkward young lovers, they fumbled at fastenings, and their emotions overtook them. Passion ruled. Their lovemaking was different from ever before, as if they were trying to prove something, each to the other. Liz's surrender was complete, and Paul had never felt so much the triumphant lover. Time was suspended. "Love me, love me," he commanded, and embraced her in a frenzy of adoration.

For a long time afterward, they clung to each other. Firelight . . . candlelight . . . the gentle sound of rain on the eaves like a lovers' lullaby . . . They slept.

Paul awoke with a start. A look at his watch confirmed that they had missed their reservations. It was after nine o'clock. "We're a couple of no-shows," he told a drowsy Liz.

She rose and demurely fastened her robe. "There's always tuna fish," she said. "We'll have a kitchen picnic."

The next morning Paul pointed out that Liz should stay home since it was Saturday and Mrs. Owen would want to leave promptly at noon. There might be delays at the hospital. Liz agreed reluctantly. She wanted to be with him.

Paul liked Dr. Logan. The man had a brisk, clinical manner, but there was warmth there too. The examination was lengthy. It included a trip down the hall for X-rays. "I'll need some time to study those," Dr. Logan told him, " but either Dr. Morris or I will be in touch with you soon."

So, Paul said to himself, at least another week of waiting.

It was Dr. Morris who called Liz at the bookstore.

"Could you come by my office this afternoon around five, Mrs. Stewart?"

"Of course," Liz answered.

She was there promptly at five.

Dr. Morris came to the point with surgical swiftness. "I'm sorry to say it's bad news, Mrs. Stewart." His voice was kind but grave.

Liz waited.

"The X-rays show a sizable brain tumor."

When Liz spoke, her voice was husky but controlled. "How soon will the operation be?"

The question seemed to her to hang in the air like a fog between them. The doctor's voice pierced through the fog, but his face was blurred. "It's inoperable, Mrs. Stewart."

"Then there's no hope."

"Only if you believe in miracles. Both Dr. Logan and I agree that the prognosis is negative."

Liz had the eerie feeling that they were discussing someone else. Paul's name hadn't even been mentioned. This couldn't be happening to Paul, to them.

The doctor went on, "The first decision you must make is whether or not Paul should be told. That's why I talked to you first." He waited.

There was no doubt in Liz's mind, and yet she found it difficult to speak, as if her answer would be a sort of death sentence. Finally she said, "Paul must be told. But when? How long does he have?"

Dr. Morris shook his head. "That's impossible to say with complete certainty, but from what we know now and what we have observed, I would predict three months at the most."

Liz's mind teemed with questions. Would the pain increase? Would Paul need to go to the hospital? Could there be a remission? Wasn't there some sort of treatment they could try, some way they could buy extra time?

Dr. Morris did his best to answer her questions one by one. Medication could keep the pain under control. There was no need for hospitalization now, perhaps not at all. Remission was doubtful, but possible. "When we talk to Paul," Dr. Morris continued, "I will suggest a procedure of treatment. I won't delude Paul with false hope, I promise you, but I would suggest that at first we do not stress the inevitable or mention the matter of time."

So Paul was told. He and Liz sat in Dr. Morris's office the next day and listened as the doctor described his case. Paul leaned slightly forward as if straining to hear words he could not believe. Dr. Morris discussed the possibility of a remission. Paul was to come to his office twice a week for treatment and to continue his medication. For the next month at least, he would suggest that life for Paul should continue its normal pattern. After that, they would see how he was reacting to the treatment. He did not take away all hope, but in his unwavering, concerned gaze and in what he left unsaid as much as what he *did* say, Paul sensed the truth of the matter.

On the way home, Liz suggested it might be a good idea to stop at some unfamiliar bar—one that had no memories for them and where they would see no one they knew. Paul agreed.

Over drinks in a newly opened tavern called The Place, they reached a number of decisions. For the next month they would work at this thing by themselves, telling neither friends nor family. Paul would continue going to the office and she would appear at Wade's Bookstore as usual. They plotted what they would do and what they would say like two actors discussing a new play in which they were to appear. They both felt the unreality of the situation, and as they had a second drink, they found themselves talking about irrelevant things.

"Like if we don't talk about it," Paul remarked suddenly, "it will go away."

Liz took his hand in hers and squeezed it hard. "Paul, I'm so proud of you, of your strength and your courage."

He smiled. "Not really tested yet."

Her eyes glistened. "Let's make this the most beautiful month of our lives. We can if we try."

"With you," Paul said quietly, "I can do anything."

In many ways it was a preposterous month. The secret they shared was so awesome that it was almost too big to comprehend. They pushed it as far back in their minds as possible. The weekends, in particular, became adventures.

Late fall can be beautiful in Illinois, and this year was no exception. Their first weekend, they "bribed" Mrs. Owen to forgo her Saturday and Sunday time off and drove to New Salem State Park. Paul had always wanted to see the reconstructed village where Lincoln had lived as a young man, but somehow he'd never made the trip. There's always tomorrow, he'd thought. Now suddenly the tomorrows were few and precious. They visited the old copper barrel shop where Lincoln had studied at night and the tavern and store in which he had been a partner. Somehow going back in time was comforting. Their interest in Lincoln was so evident that as they were leaving, a guide asked them, "Have you been to Springfield yet?"

They told him they hadn't.

"His house there is most interesting, and the tomb

is something to see," the guide assured them.

"No tombs for me," Paul responded, and grinned like a small boy at his own outrageousness.

Liz made a face at him, amazed that he could find even a ray of humor at a time like this, and yet pleased that he could.

They had never been so close. At home in the frosty evenings, they took long walks, saying little, and yet so conscious of the world about them—the glow of the full moon, the rustle of fallen leaves, the tangy, cidery smell of fall. *Savoring*, thought Liz, *we're savoring the things we once took so much for granted*.

Frequently they had friends in for drinks and conversations that avoided the personal and ranged from the Vietnamese situation to the pros and cons of the Nixon administration.

They begged off accepting Ellen and David's Thanksgiving invitation and fabricated a reunion with friends of Liz who would be in Chicago that weekend. Would the Stewarts consider looking after Betsy? Mrs. Owen would be on hand Thursday and Friday. Only Saturday and Sunday would be the problem. The Stewarts agreed.

So it would be Chicago for the holiday weekend— the end of their "most beautiful month."

Paul had made reservations at the lovely, stately Palmer House. Their Thanksgiving dinner was superb. After coffee and brandy, Liz said, "I feel like a stuffed turkey myself. Let's walk off a pound or two and look at the store windows."

Paul hesitated. "I'm still tired from the drive, and 'Baby, it's cold outside.'" He shivered.

Liz didn't insist.

Next day at the chrysanthemum show in the

Garfield Park Conservatory, he complained that all the flowers must be stirring up his allergies. "Breathing is downright difficult," he said. "Let's sit and rest for a moment."

In their hotel room Liz suggested that they cancel their theater plans for that night. "Only if we can change the tickets to Saturday night," Paul answered. They could and did. Paul seemed grateful.

"Let's be absolutely luxurious," Liz proposed, "and have dinner in our room."

"With champagne," Paul added.

As they were finishing the last of the champagne, Liz said, "Listen!" Even over the soft music from the radio they could hear the rain beating against the windows. Chicago's annual Thanksgiving storm had just been a day late in its arrival.

"The Windy City is talking to us," Paul informed her.

"What's it saying, Paul?"

"It's saying that Paul is very tired." He smiled wanly.

While he got ready for bed, Liz rang for room service to clear the dinner things away. When she went to bed, she thought he was sleeping, but as she reached to turn off the bedside lamp, he opened his eyes.

"I want to go home, Liz," he said simply.

They checked out of the hotel early on Saturday. Liz drove and Paul slept most of the way home. Now and then he opened his eyes. "I'm feeling more rested," he told her.

"We'll scoot in quietly, and no one will know we're home early," Liz told him. "You can relax, and then sometime on Sunday I'll pick up Betsy."

The plan worked perfectly. No one realized they had cut their trip short.

Paul had a Monday appointment with Dr. Morris.

Liz phoned her assistant at the bookstore and told her she would be in late. She wanted to be with Paul.

When Dr. Morris had finished his examination, he called Liz into his office and turned to both of them. "I think, Paul, that you should start taking things easy. No more going to the office. Stay home. Putter around a bit. Rest a lot."

"You mean," Paul said evenly, "become a semi-invalid."

"Not yet," Dr. Morris told him. "Just conserve your strength."

On the way home, Paul and Liz decided that they would wait until after Christmas to break the bad news to family and friends. At the office he would announce immediately that he was giving himself a month's vacation. Explanations wouldn't be necessary.

The pre-holiday weeks were busy at the bookstore. Business had never been so good. Liz hired an extra clerk. Although she went in every day, she got there later than usual and did her best to leave early.

Without being told, Mrs. Owen sensed that Paul needed more attention. She was solicitous almost to the point of hovering. His favorite desserts appeared regularly. She fussed at him to rest more. She bought a beautiful poinsettia. "A family Christmas gift," she said, but she put it in Paul's room.

Paul had always loved to read and Liz trooped in almost every day with a book that she thought would interest him. "You're a traveling library," he told her. "Such service." But when she returned in the late afternoon she noticed increasingly how often he was asleep with the open book in his lap.

He insisted that they must have a Christmas tree for Betsy. "Very well," said Liz, "but it must be a Betsy-

35

sized Christmas tree." They drove to a nearby Christmas tree farm and found exactly what they had in mind. When they returned home, they hid it in the garage. On the Sunday before Christmas, they arranged for Betsy to visit a little girl across the street. Then they brought the tree in and started decorating it.

Outside a light snow was falling. Inside the piney smell of the little tree filled the room. As they hung the tree ornaments, they recalled other Christmases. Liz placed the silver star on the tip of the tree and turned to Paul. "There's something I very much want to say, but I don't know how to say it," she began.

Paul hooked a bright red bell on one of the branches. "Try," he said.

Liz took a deep breath. "I think it's important that you and Dan reconcile. For both of you."

He started to speak.

"Hear me out," she said. "He's never been back to the bookstore. I haven't seen or talked to him. I just feel so strongly, dear, that both of you should get together. And it should be before we tell the family about your condition. Paul, it will bring you more peace of mind, and Dan, too."

He hung another bell on the tree. It made a tinkling sound. She noticed that his hand trembled.

"Call him, Paul. Make the first move. I'm confident that he'll respond."

"You call. It's your idea." Paul's voice wasn't angry, but it was noncommittal.

As she went toward the phone, she prayed that Susan wouldn't answer. She dialed and waited. Her prayer was answered. At the other end of the line, Dan said, "Hello."

"Dan, this is Liz. Paul and I have just finished

decorating the Christmas tree. Could you join us for a drink and admire our handiwork?"

There was a pause.

Liz tried to keep the urgency out of her voice. "It's important, Dan. We both want to see you." She waited for his response.

Replacing the receiver, she turned and smiled at Paul. "He's coming over," she told him, "in an hour or so."

Quickly Liz prepared Betsy's supper. She collected her from across the street and brought her into the house through the back door. After Betsy had finished her meal and had an extra cookie because she had been such a good girl, Paul disappeared. In a minute he called to them. "Now! Come see!"

Liz ushered Betsy into the living room. The tree lights twinkled. The ornaments shone in the reflected light. Betsy clapped her hands in wonder. Paul held her in his lap and told her a Christmas tree story, and then Liz took her off to bed.

They waited for Dan.

"He's decided not to come," Paul said, and went to the bar and made them drinks. They sipped at their drinks and nibbled at the appetizers Liz had prepared. Although it had grown dark, the falling snow produced a twilight effect. The room was softly bathed with light from the tree and the mantel candles. "I should have built a fire," Paul said, remembering another night of firelight and candlelight.

They heard Dan's car turn into the driveway.

He stood in the doorway with a large basket in his arms. "Presents for Betsy," he explained. "Maybe you should hide them until Christmas morning. They're all from Santa Claus."

Liz took the presents and left the two men in the

living room. She knew they needed to talk.

Paul took his adopted brother's coat and hat. When he came back, Dan said, "Beautiful tree."

"Small, like Betsy," Paul remarked. "Let's see. It's bourbon and water, isn't it? And easy on the water." He smiled.

"Correct," Dan said.

They made more pleasantries, stared at their drinks, and waited for Liz. "How's Susan?" Paul asked.

Dan shrugged. "Susan is Susan-like," he answered. His wife was not a favorite topic of conversation.

Paul cleared his throat. It was evident that Liz had decided to absent herself for awhile. The stage was theirs alone. His eyes searched Dan's face. There was still a certain boyishness about it—an open face, eager and responsive, and now it wore a quizzical look as Dan waited for Paul to speak.

When he did, the words came slowly, chosen carefully. "We've been through a lot together, Dan. We've both made mistakes, but the being together is what adds up to the most important thing." His gaze shifted from Dan. It was as if he had wandered away for a moment into a secret place of memories. Then he continued, "I'm hoping, Dan, that we can be friends again. For our happiness, for Betsy's, and for Liz, too."

Dan rose slowly and stood before Paul. He wanted to speak, but the words wouldn't come. Paul rose, too. They stood facing each other. And suddenly Dan reached out to Paul. He put his arms around him and held him in a bear-like hug. There was no need for words. They were together again.

When Liz came into the room moments later, they were discussing Christmas plans. Dan and Susan would be spending the holiday with relatives of Susan's. Paul and Liz were having Christmas dinner with Ellen and David. One look at them and Liz knew that things were right again. She gazed at the star on the Christmas tree. It shone more brightly than she remembered. Peace and good will, she thought to herself, and raised her glass in a silent toast.

Christmas was the usual flurry of excitement. The day was cold, clear, and beautiful—blue sky above white snow. "It looks so Currier and Ives," Liz said as they drove to the elder Stewarts.

Ellen had outdone herself. There was turkey with all the trimmings and, specially for Liz, an English plum pudding. With all the exclamations attending the gift exchanges, the chatter and the gaiety, Liz hoped that no one else noticed how little Paul ate, how quiet he was, and how dark were the circles under his somber blue eyes. They left early, pointing out that it had been such a big day for Betsy that they must get her to bed early.

Since Christmas was on Thursday, Liz had closed the bookstore for a long weekend—time enough on Monday to start the weary business of exchanges and returns, rejacketing of books, and preparing the monthly bills. It was just a few minutes after ten in the morning when the phone rang. It was Ellen.

"Is Paul around?" she asked.

"He's sleeping off all the Christmas excitement. Time he was up, though. Shall I call him?"

"No, no." Ellen's voice edged with anxiety, hurried on. "Liz, we're worried about Paul. He looks bad. He scarcely touched his food. What's the matter?"

For a moment Liz hesitated. Then—it will be easier this way for Paul, she thought. She told Ellen, carefully and calmly, of the hopelessness of Paul's illness. She explained why Paul and she had held back the truth until after Christmas. "It's time now that those we love must know."

Ellen's voice was steady, compassionate. "How can we help?"

"Would you tell Dan? And be sure that he knows that we told no one until just now." She paused. "You know that they're friends, like brothers . . .again?"

"Yes," Ellen replied. "Dan told me. He was so happy. Oh, Liz, this is so unfair." She hung up suddenly, unable to go on.

Soon after the new year began, Paul suffered a hemorrhage. By the time the ambulance arrived, he was in a coma. As they sped to the hospital, Liz prayed, "Please, Lord, make it quick."

Both Dr. Logan and Dr. Morris were waiting there. After their examination, they met with Liz. "He's beyond pain," they told her. "There's nothing to do but wait."

She sat by the side of the bed and studied Paul's pale, drawn face. He had fought valiantly, she thought, and though he had not won, he had found love and understanding and peace. Now, without him, would she?

He died without regaining consciousness.

Chapter Four
Condolences

According to custom, Liz and Ellen and David received friends at the Oakdale Funeral Home the night before Paul's funeral. It was a blustery, cold, wintry night. The elder Stewarts picked up Liz at her home and they stopped at a nearby restaurant for a bite to eat before going to the funeral parlor. No one was really hungry. They toyed with their food. The conversation was desultory. Not until their second cup of coffee did Liz find the words she really wanted to say.

"I'm thinking of leaving Oakdale," she began. "So many memories here."

Ellen reached out and patted Liz's hand. "My advice, dear, for what it's worth, is that you should make no decisions immediately. Give yourself time to rest and think and adjust. There's no need to rush."

David Stewart nodded in agreement. "If you need any money, Liz, while you're thinking things out . . ." His voice trailed off.

"Oh, no. But thank you. Paul had considerable

insurance. The bookstore is doing quite well, but it was thoughtful of you to offer. What I'll need, as always, from time to time, are fond grandparents who will double as Betsy-sitters."

They left the restaurant and drove to the funeral home. It had begun to snow.

The funeral home was an unreal world, hushed, scented with flowers, and overly warm. Mr. Crane, the funeral director, greeted them with murmurs in which Liz could find no meaning. A faint aroma of gin and mouthwash perfumed his unctuous mouthings. He led them down a thickly carpeted hallway to a curtained parlor. The flower scent was stronger here and faint strains of sepulchral organ music weighted the air. The lighting was dim, indirect. *Everything is indirect*, Liz thought and found it difficult to resist a strong desire to turn and find the nearest exit that led to the outdoors, to feel the fresh coolness of snow on her face.

An assistant appeared from the shadows and took their wraps. Mr. Crane was talking. "Would you prefer to greet your friends from the privacy of the alcove? It provides a focus and is less tiring."

"We'll wait here near the entrance, at least at first," Liz said.

"As you wish." There was a note of disappointment in his voice.

Ellen spoke, almost in a whisper. "Didn't you ask that the coffin be closed, Liz?" She indicated the heavily brocaded casket at the far end of the room, nearly concealed by floral arrangements.

For the first time Liz gave it her attention. She was surprised at the many flowers. The funeral notice had suggested that in lieu of flowers, contributions to the American Cancer Society would be appreciated. She was even more surprised at the dark blue ornateness of the coffin. This was not what she'd selected.

"Before I close the casket," Mr. Crane was intoning, "would you care to . . ." His question was never finished.

Quickly Liz advanced to the opened casket and looked at the figure reclining on a billowy satin field. "That isn't Paul!" she exclaimed. Mr. Crane was at her side.

"Mrs. Liston," he said, "you're upset."

Ellen and David had followed him. "Stewart," David informed him. "We're the Stewarts."

Mr. Crane looked stricken. It appeared that he was about to crumple. By now his assistant was beside him. His face was flushed. "Mr. Stewart is in the Oval Room. It was larger. I misinformed you."

With effort, Mr. Crane regained a semblance of his composure. His apologies were profuse.

Liz fought a wild urge to laugh, hysterically perhaps, but to laugh. Her lips trembled. "It's all right," she said.

"Follow me," said Mr. Crane, and once more they filed silently down the hall. At the doorway, they paused.

"You will be sure," David Stewart said icily, "that our friends are directed correctly."

Mr. Crane accepted the rebuke with as much aplomb as he could muster. "Please don't worry. This has never happened before, nor will it happen again."

The Oval Room was larger than the other. The gray, metallic casket across the room was closed. A cluster of red and white poinsettias had been placed at the head of the coffin, nothing more. It was quite unreal, but much better, Liz thought. Mr. Crane still was at her elbow. "Forgive me," said Liz, "but, yes, I think we would like to be with Paul for a moment—alone." She wanted to say, "To be sure it's Paul," but she refrained. There was no point in shattering the little man completely.

"Of course," Mr. Crane said in a hushed tone. He opened the casket and silently retreated to the far edge of the room.

It was Paul, younger-looking somehow. He appeared to be smiling ever so slightly. How he would have laughed at the mix-up, Liz thought, not at their momentary distress, but at Mr. Crane's discomfort. She hoped that somehow, somewhere nearby, he had been watching.

The three of them, Liz, Ellen, and David, stood there a minute or two longer. They said nothing, each in their ways communicating with Paul through their memories.

There was a discreet cough behind them. Mr. Crane had reappeared. "Friends are arriving," he said.

Liz indicated that he should close the casket. They stationed themselves near the doorway and greeted the first of the arrivals.

Since the night was snowy, with the prediction of a blizzard on the way, Liz had expected that only a few of their closest friends would come by. She was wrong. By eight o'clock the room was crowded, and there was a babble of voices. Some of the people, old friends of the elder Stewarts, Liz knew only slightly. There were schoolmates of Paul's whom she had heard him mention but had never met. There were people from Paul's office, old acquaintances, new acquaintances, and everyone sought to share special memories of Paul with them. It was heartwarming, confusing and tiring. Eventually, to the delight of Mr. Crane, they decided to heed his suggestion and retire to the alcove where people, a few at a time, could come by to express their sympathy.

It was here that Nancy and Chris Hughes, longtime friends of Ellen and David Stewart, found them. Ellen had known Chris Hughes as long as she could remember. He had gone to work for her grandfather, Judge Lowell, in his law firm, and now many, many years later was head of the firm. He was, in the truest sense of the phrase, a pillar of the community of Oakdale. Nancy, his wife, was one of the most gracious ladies Ellen had ever known, and she had grown up with the Hugheses' son Bob, who was only four years older than she was.

The Hugheses were speaking of Bob now. "He's coming by later and bringing his son Tom, who has just returned from Vietnam." Nancy Hughes turned to Liz. "Tom always looked up to Paul," she said. "He was so kind to Tom. To have an older boy pay so much attention to him meant a lot to him." Fleetingly, a look of unhappiness clouded Nancy's face. Liz sensed that their grandson was still a source of worry.

Oh, yes, Liz remembered now. Nancy had practically raised Tom after Bob's wife divorced him and fled to Chicago. Lisa, that was her name. Paul seldom criticized people, but even as a child, he'd found Lisa disturbing, threatening somehow.

Nancy was saying that they must be leaving now to make room for others. "It's such a tribute to Paul. So many here." They left as other friends entered to express condolences.

It was perhaps fifteen minutes later that Bob Hughes appeared. With him was a tall, gangling boy whom he introduced to Liz as his son Tom. The boy looked so young and so vulnerable that Liz's heart went out to him. So it was youngsters like this who had been fighting the strange, unpopular, faraway war in Vietnam. She tried to make him feel more at ease, but it was difficult.

He answered her questions in monosyllables, and when she told him that Paul had often mentioned him, which strictly speaking wasn't true, he stared at her expressionlessly and made no comment. Ellen and David had no better luck in engaging him in conversation. He was almost abrupt with them. It was clear that he wanted to break away. Moments later he tapped his father on the shoulder. "Gotta split now, Dad. See you later back at the house."

"But I thought . . ." Bob Hughes began, but his son had turned and walked away quickly, without so much as a goodbye to the Stewarts or to Liz.

Bob apologized for him. "Tom's having a difficult time adjusting to Oakdale once again after Vietnam." He looked directly at Ellen and David. "Let's face it," he said, "Tom has always had a difficult time. The Vietnam experience hasn't helped matters. He's all nerves. I don't know how to handle this phase." A look of pain crossed his face. "But I shouldn't worry you with our troubles," he concluded embarrassedly.

"If there's anything we can do," Ellen said, "let us know. Is Tom looking for a job?"

"Maybe I could help," David Stewart said.

"He's just drifting at present," Bob said. "Once he settles down, once he finds himself, he may give you a call." He smiled. "I'm the one who should be saying, 'Is there anything I can do for you?'" He backed away as others came in.

They were friends of the elder Stewarts and Liz knew them only slightly. She accepted their condolences and then excused herself. It was time to mingle again. Besides, some of the early arrivals were beginning to leave. The crowd was thinning out a bit. Fragments of conversation floated about her. The oft-repeated "So sorry," and "We're so saddened," echoed and echoed in her ears. She found herself responding mechanically to expressions she knew were sincere and heartfelt.

Where is Dan? she asked herself. Isn't he going to come by? She felt the need of his strength, his comforting assurance. It seemed strange that he hadn't even called her since Paul's death.

Then she saw him just entering. Was it his tallness, his instinctive interest in others that seemed to make him the center of attention? Or was it just in her mind that he was so outstanding? Now and then he stopped to greet a friend. Behind him was Susan, his wife. Her face was flushed, her mouth almost grim. They've had a fight, thought Liz. She isn't here because she wants to be—it's because Dan said she must be. Both of them had stopped to speak to Bob Hughes on his way out. Susan's gaze, ever on the alert, swept the room, and then fastened on Liz. Her eyes narrowed and darkened. *Oh, how she hates me*, Liz thought. She returned Susan's cold, distrustful look with what she hoped was an understanding expression. Of course, it wasn't easy for Susan to express condolences to Betsy's mother, to be reminded once again that Betsy was Dan's daughter, that Paul had stepped in and married Liz and adopted Betsy, had given her love and the Stewart name legally, which Susan had prevented Dan from doing.

For a moment Liz considered retiring to the alcove. Perhaps it would be easier to face Susan with Ellen and David Stewart by her side, but it was too late. Dan had spotted her and was approaching. A defiant Susan was by his side.

"Liz," he said, his firm but gentle voice warm and compassionate. His embrace revived her sagging spirits. "Mother called me. I was out of town at a meeting, you know."

Liz nodded. She hadn't known, but it didn't matter. Had someone forgotten to tell her? So what! The important thing was that he was here now.

Susan extended a cold, limp hand. "What can I say that hasn't already been said?" she asked.

Liz smiled and released her hand. "Is it still snowing? It must be getting colder."

"The snow has stopped," Dan answered. "I'm hoping the blizzard prediction is wrong."

"I'm sure that Liz could handle a little thing like weather complications," Susan remarked.

I'm not going to spar with her, Liz decided. She turned to Dan. "I'm glad you got to see Bob Hughes, but you missed his son Tom. He left earlier."

"Where are Ellen and David?" Susan inquired.

Liz pointed to the alcove.

"It's getting late, and I know they must be exhausted. Let's say good night to them. Maybe people will take the hint and leave." Susan's words were detached, without warmth. She started toward the alcove. "Are you coming with me?" It was more of a command to Dan than a question.

"I want to talk a minute more to Liz," he said.

Susan frowned and walked away.

"Betsy?" Dan asked. "Where's Betsy?"

"Mrs. Owen has a sister who lives close by. She and Betsy are there for a few days."

"Have you told Betsy about Paul?"

"She senses something is wrong. Later when there's more time, I'll try to explain," Liz said.

"Mrs. Owen won't say anything like, 'Your daddy's

gone away for a while,' or 'Daddy's asleep'?"

"Oh, no," Liz assured him. "I told her if Betsy asked questions just to tell her that she'd have to wait for her mother to answer them. But she's so young, Dan. Don't worry."

"I want to see her more often," Dan said. "I can't replace Paul, but I can show her a father's love in little ways."

Some late arrivals edged up to them with sympathetic looks and words, and then drifted away to the alcove.

"After the funeral—when it's convenient—I want to talk to you, Liz. Should I call you at home? At the bookstore?"

"I'll be at the bookstore after the first of the week. Why don't you drop by?"

"Fine," he said. "I'll see the folks now."

Liz stood by the door and thanked friends for coming. Mr. Crane was in the hallway with the look of a man who was ready to close shop for the night.

After the last of their friends had left, Liz returned to the alcove to join Ellen, David, Dan and Susan. "All gone," she said, "except Mr. Crane, who is waiting for us to leave." She noticed that someone had already brought their coats. They started to put them on. Liz addressed Dan and Susan. "Tomorrow after the funeral our neighbors are serving lunch." She nodded to Ellen and David. "You'll be there, I know, and Dan and Susan, you'll join us, I hope."

"Of course," Dan said.

"I should have told you," Susan remarked, "that I won't be at the funeral." There was no regret in her voice.

Dan looked as surprised as the rest of them.

"It's my day at the clinic. I'll be there all day," Susan

said, with an evident absence of regret.

"But couldn't you join us for lunch?" Ellen asked.

Susan shook her head. "It's quite impossible." She looked at Liz almost challengingly. "There'll be so many there, I'm sure I won't be missed."

Mr. Crane was in the doorway. He cleared his throat. "Is there anything more I can do?"

"We're just leaving," Liz told him. "Thank you, Mr. Crane."

"The limousine will pick you up at ten-thirty," he said. Liz and the elder Stewarts nodded agreement.

Outside the cold air was like a tonic. A pale moon gave a luminous quality to the drifted snow. Mr. Crane's assistant was clearing the sidewalk. "I brushed the snow from your windshields," he called.

They thanked him and walked on to the cars. Dan stopped and hugged the Stewarts and Liz. Susan called to him from their car. "Come on, Dan. I'm freezing."

Liz climbed into the Stewarts' car. As they drove over the snowy road, Ellen said, "Please spend the night with us, Liz."

The invitation was tempting. Liz dreaded the thought of the empty house waiting for her, but this was something she must face—the sooner, the easier. "Thank you, but no. I'll be fine."

"Then promise you'll join us for coffee and breakfast rolls," Ellen said. "Our neighbors have been generous, too. So much food!"

"I'll be there by nine," Liz answered.

They reached her house. Some thoughtful neighbor had already shoveled the walk clean. David saw her to the door. "Good night, Liz. You're a strong, brave woman, but let us help however we can."

She squeezed his hand. "Of course." She reached

into her purse for the keys. "You can start now by unlocking the door. I'm such a fumbler with keys."

There was no need to explain that her eyes, suddenly misted with tears, could not even see the keyhole. She waved a quick goodbye and entered the silent house. *Tomorrow*, she thought, *will be the longest day of my life.* Then resolutely she squared her shoulders and climbed the stairs to the bedroom.

Chapter Five
An Argument

The limousine appeared precisely at ten-thirty, as Mr. Crane had promised. Liz was waiting with Ellen and David. It was a cold, clear day. The blizzard had not materialized. As they rode to the church, Ellen thought, *Liz looks less tense this morning, more determined and calm, somehow.*

Liz spoke, and it seemed as though she had been reading Ellen's thoughts. "I'm more at peace with myself," she said. "I know you advised against hasty decisions and I thought some things through last night." She paused. "I'm not leaving Oakdale. How could I leave friends and the only family I've known? How could I turn over Wade's Bookstore to someone else?"

Ellen smiled. "Oh, I'm glad, Liz. This is where you belong."

"Home is where the heart is," Liz quoted, "and my heart is here."

"You've made a good decision," David told her. "One you won't regret."

For no apparent reason, Liz shivered. She couldn't explain it. It was as if a wordless premonition shadowed her decision with a cloud of doubt. Are you sure, Liz? Leave Oakdale before it's too late. Paul's voice? Dan's? She was imagining things.

The ordeal of the funeral was not as bad as Liz had expected. Both Ellen and Liz had asked for familiar psalms, and the words had a comforting ring.

Liz had always taken religion for granted. It was part of life's pattern, but rather indefinable. Now the words of the psalmist took on a deeper meaning.

The cemetery was high on a hill, and it was bitterly cold. Many of those moments were only a blur to Liz, but the words of the psalms still sustained her.

Once they had returned home, it was reality again. The familiar faces of friends and neighbors were kind and warm. And there were practical questions to answer.

"Where do you keep the sugar, Liz?"

"Do you have an extension cord for the coffee maker?"

The Hugheses, Nancy and Chris, were there. Ellen had asked that they join them. Liz was surprised to see Bob Hughes there, as well, with his son Tom. Someone had provided a large pitcher of Bloody Marys, and Liz asked their next-door neighbor, Fred Zilling, if he would be bartender. She saw Bob Hughes frown as Fred handed a generous Scotch on the rocks to Tom. Once again Liz thought, *There's a problem there*, but she was too busy to think more about it.

Dan had unconsciously assumed the role of surrogate host. His very presence was reassuring, and he moved from group to group, skillfully putting people at ease, introducing the few who did not know each other. At one point Liz noticed him in earnest conversation with the young Tom Hughes. The boy was smiling. *Dan can win over anyone*, Liz thought; and then, noticing the boy's flushed face, she decided that the Scotch might have had a part in breaking down his defenses.

The ladies of the kitchen were at her side. "We're ready to serve. Perhaps if you'll start, others will follow."

Then finally people were leaving. Tom Hughes was one of the first to leave, but this time he did seek out Liz to murmur embarrassed thanks. "I thought a lot of Paul, you know," he said. Bob was at his side. Tom turned a bit unsteadily to his father. "You don't have to go now, Dad. I can hoof it. It's not all that far."

"The walk might do you good," Bob said.

The boy looked at him impassively and then strode out of the room.

It was late afternoon before Bob returned home. After leaving Liz and Ellen and David, he drove by Memorial Hospital. There were a couple of patients he wanted to check and he needed to review his schedule for the coming day. When he finally drove into his driveway, the house was dark. For a moment, he sat in the car and thought about the afternoon. It was true that Tom had had an extra drink or two at Liz's, but it had been wrong to embarrass the boy in front of others. He would suggest that they go out for dinner and have a heart-to-heart talk. The boy needed understanding and advice. He knew that Tom was seeing his mother from time to time, but Bob seriously doubted that Lisa was being helpful. She was too preoccupied with her own interests and her very young son Chuckie. Most likely she would dole out some money to Tom and hurry him away. Tom must be a source of guilt to her, just as he was to Bob. But at least he had stood by and tried to raise his son. Lisa had run away and now that she was back in Oakdale, the memories she stirred up were difficult for Bob. All very well to say, "Let bygones be bygones," Bob thought, but it wasn't easy. And it couldn't be easy for Tom. He sighed and walked toward the house.

Switching on lights, he called to his son.

There was no answer.

"Tom," he called again.

There was a muffled response from the den. He found Tom there sitting in the dark, a drink in his hand. "Let's have a little light on the subject," Bob said jovially.

"Poor joke, Dad."

Bob ignored the comment. "How about my joining you, and then let's go out and find a thick, juicy steak?"

Tom waved toward the bar. "Help yourself. It's all yours." He emphasized the last word.

Bob poured himself a drink and sat across from Tom. "Glad to see you having a good talk with Dan Stewart at Liz's. So many good friends there. I'm sure Liz appreciated all the kindness and love."

"Quite a ritual," Tom observed.

"But rituals can be useful," Bob remarked. "They occupy the mind, divert it. A kind of therapy. And they serve as a way for people to indicate feelings too deep to express."

Tom mixed himself another drink. "Most of the jerks acted as though they were at a party. Let's have a ball now that we've got good old Paul stashed away."

I'm not going to get into an argument with him, Bob told himself. "Oakdale is a close community. People reach out to help one another."

Tom laughed. "They help themselves to each other's

wives and husbands. The Oakdale Trading Post!"

"Tom!" Bob's voice was sharper than he meant it to be.

"Oh, Dad, don't be such a romantic. This is a gossipy, hypocritical, stuck-up small town. You only see what you want to see, remember what you want to remember."

Bob tried to interrupt.

"Look it square in the face, Dad. You, a doctor, of all people, should know the lies, the slander, who's sleeping with who." He gulped his drink. "Take our own poor excuse for a family. Grandma pretending all's right with the world when Mom runs out on me. You and your miserable marriage to jailbird Sandy, leaving me with Grandma while you panted after her. You got your Sandy and I got her miserable son Jimmy." He mimicked his father's voice. "'And now you'll have a brother, Tom.'"

"That's enough," Bob said.

Tom disregarded his words. "And how about Mom's little Chuckie, my sweet baby bastard half-brother? How do you think I feel about that? Is it any wonder I want to leave Oakdale?"

Once more he was at the bar. "Oh, Dad, face facts for a change."

Bob spoke quietly. "And I suppose you think you're facing facts. Where do you find them—at the bottom of the bottle? Was running away to the army facing facts? Yes, I'm a doctor. I understand what you're going through. But drink—" he paused—"and—drugs— won't solve a thing, Tom. Let me help."

Tom focused on his father with difficulty. "I don't want a sermon, Dad. I don't need psalms read to calm and comfort me. Poor Tommy," he said in mock despair, "always Daddy's little problem. And now he's

Daddy's big problem. A steak? A sermon? That ain't gonna solve this problem, Daddy-boy."

"Neither will another slug," Bob said as Tom turned toward the bar again.

They were both on their feet.

"Tom, I'm sorry. Let's begin again from the start."

Tom shook his head. "Not tonight, Dad." Then suddenly he was like a little boy again, wheedling, the quick shift of moods that had always so perplexed Bob. "Gimme the car keys, Dad, please. I need to ride around and cool off."

For the boy's safety and for others, he couldn't do it, even though it would mean a temporary peace treaty. "Sorry, Tom. You've had too much to drink."

He was the spoiled brat, denied what he wanted most, for the moment. "Damn it! I'm not a child. I know what I'm doing."

"No, Tom."

Tom started crying, but they were tears of anger and frustration.

Bob reached out to put his arms around him, but Tom backed off.

"Then I know where I can get a car. Mom will lend me one of hers. Good old Mom, who tries so hard to make up for so much!" He flung on his coat and lurched out of the house.

I must call Lisa, Bob thought. *I must tell her she can't let Tom have a car, that he's in no condition to drive.* As he dialed her number, he wondered if Lisa would listen to him. Would she give Tom the car just to spite her ex-husband?

The insistent buzz announced that the line was busy. He swore. Her line was always busy! For a couple of minutes he waited, and then he dialed again. Still the buzz.

Tom paused a few seconds outside Lisa's house to regain his breath. He had run most of the way. Leaning against one of the columns of the ornate portico, he inhaled deeply. "Sober, sober," he whispered. He rang the doorbell.

It was moments before Lisa answered. "Tom!" Her deep blue eyes seemed to look through him. "I'm sorry. I was on the phone. Come in out of the cold."

He paused in the doorway. "Mom, could I borrow your car? It's sort of an emergency. I won't be gone for long."

Lisa hesitated. Behind her the telephone rang.

"It's probably Dad," Tom said. "We had a bit of a fight, and he got huffy, the way Dad does. He's trying to punish me like a little boy."

The telephone rang again.

"Please, Mom."

She remembered the many times he'd said, "Please, Mom" as a little boy, and how she had turned her back on him. Let the telephone ring. From her pocketbook she extracted the car keys. "The car's in the driveway."

Unexpectedly, he gave her a kiss. His breath was heavy with alcohol. "Tom," she called, but he was down the steps and into the car. He gunned it and backed too quickly down the driveway, skidding a bit where the melted snow had now formed ice patches. "Tom!" But he was gone.

The phone was ringing again. Well, she wasn't going to answer it and have Bob criticize her for lending her car to Tom. She hoped the insistent ringing would not wake up Chuckie. He was a difficult little boy to get to sleep. When the telephone stopped ringing, she took the receiver off the hook. Deliberately, she switched off all the lights downstairs. She would read in the sun parlor at the back of the house until she was sleepy. If

Bob came by, the house would be dark.

Bob didn't try to call Lisa again. He told himself that she might not be at home. He waited a little while to see if Tom came back. *It's no good staying here*, he thought. He would have a steak by himself. Later maybe he'd see a movie. Something light to take his mind off the trouble at hand. He checked the paper. *Cactus Flower* was at the Strand. That should do the trick. On the way to the restaurant, he drove by Lisa's house. It was dark. He wondered where Tom might be.

Tom didn't know exactly where he was. He had driven out of Oakdale to the open highway. There was plenty of gas. He drove with no goal in mind, trying to sort out his jumbled thoughts. Nothing seemed to add up, himself most of all. Heedless of the miles or the snow-covered flatness of the surrounding country, he drove on and on into the night. Was his dad right? Was he always trying to escape, like now, driving without direction, without any plan?

Suddenly he felt he had no energy. He needed a drink and some food. Abruptly he wheeled the car around on the four-lane highway and headed back to Oakdale. At the edge of town, he stopped at a tavern. The place was busy but not crowded. A brightly neoned jukebox blared away, and a few couples danced to the strains of "Let the Sun Shine In." He found a booth as far away from the music as he could. There was no sunshine anywhere, as far as he could tell, to let in.

"What's yer pleasure?" A heavy, bovine waitress—her gum-chewing heightened the effect—was at his side.

"Double Scotch, house Scotch." When she left, he checked his wallet. Sixteen dollars. It would cover another drink and supper at this crummy place. When he returned the car, he would ask his mom for some money. And then what? He didn't want to go home, not tonight. He felt like a little boy. *I ran away and now I'm back home, Daddy.* He sipped his drink. From the jukebox Peggy Lee began serenading him with "Is That All There Is?"

He looked around the room. There was a girl alone in a booth across the dance floor. She was pretty in a sort of underfed way. Too thin, really, and flat-chested, but friendly-looking. Maybe soon he'd ask her to dance. Another drink might help untangle his feet. He beckoned to the waitress and raised his glass. "Another one and a hamburger, well done."

He drank the second Scotch more slowly. The hamburger was okay, but he wasn't as hungry as he thought. Waiting until the girl looked his way, he raised his glass in a salute and smiled. She smiled back. *Now is the hour,* he thought. He walked carefully to her booth and bowed. "Shall we dance?"

"Don't mind if I do," she said. *Let the Sunshine In* was playing again. "I just love that song."

He held her in his arms and hesitantly, they started dancing. Never a good dancer, he found it more difficult than usual to get the beat of the music. But it was pleasant to hold her close. They made little progress, swaying more than dancing.

"What's your name?"

"Patricia, but everyone calls me Patty. Yours?"

"Tom. Thomas Miller Hughes, but everyone calls me Thomas Miller Hughes." He smiled at his little joke, tripped slightly, and held her closer. Her slight body felt good against his. Perhaps she wasn't as flat-chested as he had thought. Her warm softness excited him. He pressed harder and tripped again. This time they nearly fell to the floor.

She pulled back and looked at him angrily. "You're too drunk to dance," she said in a voice that could be overheard. "Get lost."

Deserted in the middle of the dance floor, he looked around helplessly for a minute and then stumbled to his booth. Throwing a ten-dollar bill on the table, he grabbed his coat and made his way out of the place as fast as he could. He started the car and looked at the clock on the dashboard. It wasn't quite eleven o'clock. If he hurried, his mom might still be up and he could get some money from her. He gunned the engine and roared away towards Lisa's house.

The streets were familiar, but he drove too fast. Two stoplights were green, but the third one was red. He barreled through, nevertheless, and a second later heard the siren and saw the flashing red light of a police car in his rear-view mirror. *Oh, no, not that, on top of everything else.* He cut down a side street and crossed to a wider avenue where he could pick up speed. So far, so good! He could still hear the siren, but his rear-view mirror reflected no flashing light. Perhaps he had eluded them. If he turned down the next side street, he could take a back road to his mom's place. He turned too quickly, skidded on an icy patch, and lost control. One of Oakdale's famed oaks stopped the car abruptly. His head cracked against the windshield and he lost consciousness.

The crash alerted the neighborhood. Lights came on. People hurried outside. Minutes later, the police car arrived, and one of the officers radioed for an ambulance.

They pulled the young man from the front seat. He was bleeding profusely from a gash on his forehead. Someone brought a blanket and put it over him as he lay there on the curb. A dark bruise was already showing under one eye. "Don't think he's much hurt. Just shook up. A few stitches and he should be all right." But he did not regain consciousness and as they waited, they became alarmed. There might be internal injuries. His face was as white as the snow around him.

When the ambulance arrived, he was still unconscious. Once again there was the sound of the siren and red lights flashing, but this time it was the ambulance and the police car ahead clearing the way.

Slowly, he opened his eyes and stared at the young man who was holding a compress to his forehead.

"An accident," the intern said. "Don't worry. You'll be all right."

He was still groggy, but he remembered that he had been in his mom's car. Had he totaled it?

They seemed to be riding forever, and his head throbbed painfully. "Where are we going?"

"Memorial Hospital," the intern replied.

Oh, my God! he thought, Dad's hospital.

Once again he slipped into unconsciousness.

Chapter Six
Confession

Memorial General Hospital was an imposing building. Oakdale inhabitants were justly proud of it and its reputation. The ivied brick walls gave it a college look. The hospital park surrounding it could have been mistaken for a campus. From miles around, doctors in local communities sent patients there. It attracted top-flight specialists and its research facilities were on a par with the best in the state. The staff was known for its excellence. Bob Hughes, chief of staff, was famous as a cardiologist in his own right, but he was also known as a fair and able administrator. It could be said that in a way much of Oakdale's social life revolved around the hospital. There were few lives in Oakdale not touched somehow by what went on at Memorial.

Bob Hughes had always made a point of scrupulously keeping his personal and professional lives separate. Perhaps the severest test had been when Michael Shea, whom he respected as one of the ablest doctors on his staff, had blatantly had an affair with Lisa, Bob's former wife. They eventually became the gossip of Oakdale. True, Bob and Lisa were divorced a long time ago, but still it rankled. Bob told himself that he felt that way mainly because Claire, Shea's wife, was an innocent victim. Then when Lisa became pregnant and Shea refused to divorce Claire because of her wealth and social status, Bob was profoundly revolted by his greed. When Claire had found out about the baby and threw herself in front of that truck, there still was no marriage between Lisa and Michael.

Bob had pondered this a great deal. He imagined that the independent, proud Lisa had seen Shea's true colors and refused a marriage of convenience. He knew that Lisa allowed Shea to see his son Chuckie frequently. At parties when the talk centered on the situation, Bob refused to be drawn into the discussion. All he knew was that Shea's conduct as a man was repulsive, though his performance as a doctor was satisfactory. He kept him on the staff.

The ambulance came to a stop at the hospital's emergency entrance, and Tom Hughes was wheeled in, still unconscious. When he came to, a short time later, he was lying on an examining table and a nurse was bending over him. "The doctor will be here in just a minute," she said. She smiled a noncommittal smile. "Don't try to talk. Just relax."

He couldn't repress a grin, even though it hurt. *Relax! What a joke.* He watched her as she went about her duties, methodically placing instruments on a nearby table, readying vials and bottles, checking the sterilizer. Her precise, starchy efficiency was reassuring.

When the doctor entered, the nurse changed noticeably. She all but fluttered, and her voice, cool and detached when she had said a few brief words to

Tom, now became almost honeyed. It was doctor this, and doctor that, and what can I do for you, doctor? The man was good-looking, tall, well-built on angular lines, with hair the color of burnished copper. His voice was crisp, but there was a lilt to it. There was something familiar about him. He came over to Tom and looked down at him. The deep blue eyes were large, but heavily lidded. Where had he seen that mouth before, a smaller edition perhaps, but the same slightly lopsided tilt to the smile? Chuckie, of course— that was it.

Tom was not surprised when the doctor said, "I'm Dr. Michael Shea, and, according to your billfold which the police handed in at the desk, you're Tom Hughes."

Tom nodded. So this was Chuckie's father, the man who'd charmed his mother into a disastrous affair. He wondered what Dr. Michael Shea was thinking. Surely he must know that Tom was Lisa's son.

The doctor's skillful, gentle hands were probing, pressing on Tom's face. "Does this hurt?" he asked as Tom winced slightly.

"Not much."

"You've had a nasty crack, but fortunately not much damage as far as I can tell. We'll need a few stitches here." He indicated the gash on Tom's forehead. "And we'll take an X-ray or two just to be sure." He directed the attentive nurse to prepare Tom for the stitches. "The hospital tried to call your father, but couldn't reach him."

"My mother?" Tom couldn't resist the question.

Michael Shea's answer was curt. "She didn't answer." He continued his examination. "Now an injection to deaden the pain of the stitches and while we're waiting for it to take effect, we'll check the old torso to be certain there are no cracked ribs." The man was competent and thorough. Yet there was something about him that Tom distrusted. His fingers pressed Tom's forehead. "Feel that?"

Tom shook his head.

"Then we're ready." As he stitched up the wound, Michael Shea talked on. "A couple of months and this won't show. Wouldn't want a scar on that handsome face. You're a first-rate patient, Tom."

The man did his best to ingratiate himself. Tom was surprised that his mother could have been taken in by such a performer.

"There. All done. And a neat job, if I do say so myself."

"Lovely, doctor," the nurse said.

"Thank you, Agnes. Now one of your neat bandages for dramatic effect."

As the nurse went about her handiwork, Michael Shea continued his monologue. "After Tom here has rested a bit, a couple of X-rays will be in order. I'll call the lab and order them. Take him down there, Agnes, and then bring him to my office. We'll have a little talk, Tom, about care and procedure. Now that my A-one priority patient is taken care of, I must see about the others. I leave him in your capable hands, Agnes." He smiled his quick, lopsided smile and was gone.

When she had him sit up, Tom admitted he felt a bit woozy. Agnes helped him to his feet and carefully they made their way to the X-ray lab. That taken care of, it was back to the examining room. "Just you lie here for awhile and rest," Agnes said. "I'll be back soon."

Tom closed his eyes. His mind was in a turmoil. What about his mom's car? Would he be arrested for speeding and drunken driving? He tried to empty his mind of all problems, but it was impossible. Would something like this get in the papers? Headlines blazed before his eyes—*Doctor's Son in Drunken Crash.*

He'd never be able to get a job in Oakdale now. As soon as he'd recovered from this, he would get some money from his mom and pull up stakes. Chicago! That was a good place to lose himself in. No! There he was just as his dad had said, running away again, escaping. He would stay here in Oakdale, make something of himself. He'd show them all that Tom Hughes was a responsible, successful citizen. He would find a job in spite of his reputation. Maybe go to night school. *Now you're escaping through dreams,* he told himself, but he did feel more in tune with reality. The decision to stay in Oakdale cleared the way for some definite planning.

Whatever Shea had given him to deaden the pain was wearing off. His head was beginning to throb. His throat was dust-dry, and his lips felt cracked. Why didn't Nurse Starch come back and take him to Shea's office as she'd been told to do? He ached all over. He felt nauseated. He had half a mind to try and find Shea's office himself. Surely the doctor could fix him up with something to make him feel like a human being again.

Almost on cue the nurse entered the room.

"How are we feeling, Mr. Hughes?"

"I don't know how you're feeling," Tom responded, "but I feel like hell."

She appeared not to have heard him. "Here are your personal effects."

From the small plastic bag he took his billfold, loose change, an identification bracelet, and his watch. The crystal was smashed. The hands had stopped at eleven-ten.

"Now," she said, "let's go see Dr. Shea." The name

was uttered with an air of deep reverence.

They stepped across the hall to a waiting room and then through a door to an adjoining room that was obviously Michael Shea's private office. He was nowhere to be seen. "Dr. Shea," she called softly as if to summon him from an inner sanctum. There was no answer.

For a fearful moment, Tom thought she would lead him back to the examining room. What a time to be deserted by your doctor. He looked around the office as if searching for a clue. His eyes halted at Shea's desk. "Could that be a note on his desk?" Tom asked.

The nurse picked up a piece of paper, glanced at it, and handed it to Tom. Written in small, neat, carefully formed letters, it said that Dr. Shea had been called on an emergency. *Just wait, Tom. I'll be back soon.*

"Is there anything I can get for you?" the nurse asked.

"A glass of water please. And where's the bathroom?" She indicated a door to the right. By the time she came back, Tom had relieved himself. He thanked her for the water.

"If you need anything, I'm on extension four," she said. "I'm sure Dr. Shea will be returning soon." She left, closing the door behind her.

Tom surveyed the room and Shea's desk in particular. There was the usual array of medical books and a picture of Chuckie. He leafed through one of the books. Dull, almost incomprehensible reading for him. Cautiously he opened the center drawer of Shea's desk. It was neat and organized. Prescription blanks, an address book, pens, pencils, paper clips, and labeled keys. He felt that he was invading the man's privacy, but forbidden territory though it was, he was fascinated. The address book tempted him.

What the hell! He opened it. Yes, his mom's name was there, complete with address and telephone number in Shea's small, concise, cramped handwriting. He leafed through the pages. Most of the names were those of women. A few had exclamation points after their names, and there were some intriguing addresses: Domino Club, and the comment, "Last show at 1 A.M."; and The Pines, "Don't call after 10 P.M."

Okay, he was a Peeping Tom. Where was Shea, anyway? He needed something badly to ease the pain. Closing the address book, he picked up the keys. Some of the labels were mystifying, but the one that bore the printed tag *Drugs* needed no explanation. He looked around the room. There were a number of cabinets, gray, green, yellow, white, black, red. It added an attractive color touch to the room, and then Tom noticed that the key labels were color-coded to match the cabinets. *Drugs*, for instance, must be the green cabinet.

He felt a great need for something to alleviate both the physical pain and the emotional pain that he was undergoing.

Damn it! Where was Shea?

As a doctor's son, he realized that emergency calls could never be timed with any accuracy. Evidently this one was taking longer than Shea had foreseen. He looked at the green cabinet. It would be so easy to unlock the door, grab some Quaaludes, for instance, and be fortified in the days ahead.

Vietnam had taught him how drugs could ease friction and fear. 'Ludes were not as effective as some of the stuff he had used in Vietnam, but they would serve the purpose. He who hesitates is lost, he told himself. His hand closed around the key and quickly he stepped over to the green cabinet. Success! The key eased into the lock and he opened the cabinet door. On the shelves were many containers also neatly labeled. He found the Quaaludes and permitted himself to take only a few. Shea might notice if he was too greedy, but surely he would never miss only a few 'ludes. Replacing the container, he tuned from the cabinet just as Shea opened the door. The doctor advanced quickly, if a bit warily, and held out his hand. Without a word, Tom handed him the Quaaludes and the key to the cabinet.

"Is that absolutely all you took?" Shea asked.

"Yes."

"Can I take your word for it? Or must I search you?" It was as though Shea was questioning himself.

"That's it," Tom said. "Everything. I'm sorry."

"Sorry isn't enough," Shea responded. "This is a criminal offense, Tom."

"I needed something to ease the pain. I kept thinking you'd come back . . ." He had neither the strength nor the concentration to finish the sentence.

"Sit down, Tom." Shea took a chair opposite him.

The silence between them was like a wall. They regarded each other as strangers, which in a sense they were. Tom spoke first. "I'm going through hell, Doctor. Can't you give me something? I need your help."

Michael Shea buzzed for the nurse.

She appeared right away—breathless, efficient, eager to serve.

"Mr. Hughes is having some unpleasant after-effects. I'm going to give him an injection. Would you take care of the preparations?" She instructed Tom to remove his jacket and roll up his sleeve. The acrid smell of rubbing alcohol stung his nostrils as she swabbed his arm. If either she or Michael Shea noticed needle marks, their faces remained impassive. After he had given Tom the injection, Shea dismissed the nurse. "It's long past your tour of duty. You've been most helpful. You're due some well-deserved rest."

She nearly swooned at such praise.

"I'll stay here with Mr. Hughes," Shea continued, "until he's feeling better. Please close the office—and good night."

A partial numbness enveloped Tom. He wondered what the injection had been. Shea was addressing him and though the words came through clearly enough, he was not sure that he understood them.

"I've reached your mother. She knows now that there was a minor accident and that neither you nor the car was damaged extensively. Your father has also been informed and told not to worry. Because of the lateness of the hour, you will spend what's left of the night here. Lie down on the couch. You'll sleep now for two hours or so. Later we'll have a talk." He put a pillow under Tom's head and placed a blanket over him. As he looked at Tom, whose eyes were nearly closed, Michael Shea smiled. It was a strange, almost sardonic smile. The night had been long, but it had been a good one for him. Fate had dealt him a good hand.

When he was confident that Tom was sleeping soundly, Shea went to his desk. He was a methodical man. There were plans to be made. From a drawer he took a notepad and carefully outlined his course of action for the immediate future. He read and reread what he had written, adding a few notes here and there. Then he leaned back in his chair and smiled with satisfaction. It all dovetailed neatly, a truly foolproof plan. There was one more thing to do. Convinced that Tom would not wake up, he left the room and seated himself before the nearest typewriter.

It was time for him to compose Tom's confession.

At seven o'clock, Tom was awakened by Michael Shea. "I'm off duty," Shea told him and handed him a cup of coffee. "Drink this and listen carefully to me." He was not the ingratiating Shea that Tom had seen much earlier. There was an intentness about him that almost seemed sinister. His face was unsmiling. His blue eyes were cold.

"You're in deep trouble, Tom. You broke into my drug cabinet and were apprehended with stolen drugs on your person. The police have already charged you with speeding, running a red light, damaging public property, and drunken driving."

Why this recital of known facts? Tom wondered. Did the man take sadistic pleasure in repeating what they both already knew? He looked at Shea helplessly. What did he want?

"You have a drug problem, and I would guess a problem with alcohol too."

Tom stared at the floor. Then he looked at Shea. "I'd like to go home now. I'll talk to my dad about what should be done."

"No!" Shea's voice was sharp. "Don't you see what unhappiness this would cause him? Don't you realize the shame and the sorrow Lisa would feel?"

Tom was not sure that he did. It was all so confusing. What was this to Shea, who scarcely knew him?

The doctor continued. "I'm too fond of your family and what they represent to Oakdale to let this happen."

Tom looked at him uncomprehendingly.

"I can help you, Tom." Shea moved to his side and put his arm around the boy's shoulder. His voice, no longer sharp, almost purred. "I have connections, Tom. Doctors learn a lot about people, many people, including the police and their families. A word from me to this one and to that one and I can assure you that the charges against you will be dropped."

Tom shook his head. It didn't seem right, but if there was a way out . . .

Shea went on. "The drug break-in is something else. Ethically, I'm bound to report you."

Tom waited.

"Together, Tom, I think we can solve this. Only you and I know what happened. If you swear silence, then I'll be silent too. Not a word to anyone."

Tom nodded, but what was the catch?

"I also want to protect you against yourself, Tom. I've a written confession here for you to sign. If you start taking drugs again, then I'll go to the police with your confession and press charges. If you stay clean for a year, I'll destroy it. It's your passport to a better life, Tom, and it's my guarantee that you won't fail. And, Tom, I'll help you in every way I can to break the habit."

Shea handed the paper to Tom. It didn't take the boy long to read it.

I, Thomas Miller Hughes, confess that I broke into Dr. Michael Shea's drug cabinet, having stolen keys from his desk and with deliberate intent, took a number of Quaaludes from a container so marked. Apprehended at the scene by Dr. Michael Shea when he returned to his office, I attempted to conceal the drugs, but on demand turned them over to him. At the time of the theft, I was fully conscious that such a crime was punishable by arrest and imprisonment if convicted.

Tom looked at Michael Shea. Was the man sincerely giving him a chance to escape all the charges that could be lodged against him? Everything had seemed hopeless before and now here was a way out, arranged neatly, courtesy of Michael Shea.

"Sign it, Tom. Believe me, the police charges will be dropped. The drug burglary incident will never be known, and you'll have the greatest incentive to break this deplorable habit before it takes over your life. I want to give you this chance, Tom."

He took the paper and the pen Michael Shea offered him.

"It will be our secret, Tom. Just between us. You won't regret it."

Well, what was there to lose? He took a deep breath and in his clear, bold handwriting signed the confession *Thomas Miller Hughes*.

Chapter Seven
A Double-Edged Proposal

Tom returned to his home from Memorial Hospital by taxi. On the way he planned what he would tell his father. As he had promised, he would say nothing about how Michael Shea was helping him out of this present predicament. He would first apologize for the way he had acted. He would minimize the seriousness of the accident and stress his new resolve to stay in Oakdale, find a job, and make something of his life.

Bob Hughes was in the kitchen finishing a second cup of coffee. He heard the front door open and knew it must be Tom.

"Dad!" Tom stood in the doorway. His bandaged head gave him a rakish look. He was a handsome kid, Bob thought, and at this moment he looked so vulnerable with his uncertain smile, the heavily shadowed eyes, the bruise on his cheek.

"How do you feel?" he asked his son.

"Okay. Dad, I'm sorry about last night. It won't happen again."

Bob brushed the apology aside. "What about Lisa's

car? Is it badly banged up?" he asked.

"Just a few dents, Dad. Don't worry, I'll get it fixed."

"How about some coffee?" Bob poured his son a cup and finished his own. "I have to run. I have patients waiting. You're sure you're all right?"

"Dr. Shea took good care of me, Dad. Be sure and tell him how much I appreciate all he did."

"Shea!" Bob hadn't known that Shea had been on night duty. It was ironic that Michael Shea would be the one to take care of Lisa's son. "Well, get some rest, Tom. I'll try to get home early. Shall we try again for a steak dinner somewhere?" He smiled.

"I'd like that, Dad." He helped his father on with his coat. "And, Dad . . ."

"Yes?"

"Don't worry about me. I've done some thinking since last night. I'm going to settle down and establish priorities. Tomorrow I'll start looking for a job."

Bob smiled at his son. "That's good news, Tom. That's really good news."

As he drove to Memorial, Bob Hughes hummed along with the car radio. It had been a long time since he had felt like singing.

Michael Shea felt like singing, too. He now had a trump card in Tom Hughes's signed confession, and if he played it right, he could win the game that he had in mind. He left the hospital and drove to his apartment. Three hours of sleep would be enough for him. First a shower to remove the hospital smell that seemed to penetrate even the skin. In bed he congratulated himself on the ease with which he'd been able to convince Tom Hughes that signing the confession was the thing to do. Then he was asleep, untroubled by any pangs of conscience.

By eleven he was up, dressed, and at the diner across from his apartment. "Hi, honey," he greeted the waitress with whom he automatically flirted and who loved his innuendoes as he ordered his egg "over easy" with much rolling of the eyes. He also stared pointedly at her ample bosom as he requested "one of those big soft rolls that I love so much."

He was in fine fettle as he drove to the police court. First things first. It should be easy enough to get the charges against young Tom dismissed. He had only to remind the police chief, Lem Webb, that he owed him a favor. Shea had personally attended to Webb's contusions after a brawl at the Domino Club and talked his victim out of having him charged with assault and battery, the "victim" having owed Shea a favor too.

The deal was neatly arranged with Webb. Also, at Shea's suggestion, he saw to it that Lisa's car, which had been impounded, would be turned over to Shea.

Fine so far. It was only a little after one o'clock and Shea was ready for the second phase of his plan. He drove Lisa's battered car to Logan's Garage. Logan did all Shea's automobile servicing very reasonably, ever since the doctor had privately handled an abortion for Logan's girlfriend.

"The fender's no problem," Logan told him. "A new windshield and radiator will take a while longer."

"I'm in a big rush, Mac. How's Goldie these days?" Goldie was Logan's girlfriend.

"Jes' fine, doc. Have it fixed up like new by the end of the week."

Shea looked crestfallen. "By the way, Mrs. Logan is responding nicely to the back treatments. I'll be seeing her again on Friday."

"I'll try my best to have the car ready for you by late

tomorrow afternoon, doc," Logan promised.

"Now you're talking," Shea said and gave him a friendly pat on the shoulder. "I'll be around by five to pick it up. Let me know any time you need another favor, Mac. Anybody here who can give me a lift to the hospital?"

At the hospital, Shea rounded up reports on a couple of cases he could discuss with Bob Hughes. They were enough out of the routine to serve as good excuses to see Hughes. He called Hughes's office. "This is Dr. Shea. Could I see Dr. Hughes sometime this afternoon? A couple of cases I want to discuss with him."

"Just a minute, Dr. Shea." And then "How about four o'clock?"

"Splendid."

Bob Hughes did not keep Shea waiting. He greeted him with a smile. "I want to thank you for taking such good care of Tom."

"Glad I could help out," Shea responded. "He's a nice kid." He discussed the two cases with Hughes. As he started to leave the office, he paused. "In case Tom is job-hunting, I might be able to help him."

"That's very nice of you."

"And by the way, it's about time for my review to be coming up. I want you to know that I'm very happy here at Memorial."

He turned and left.

When Shea got back to his apartment, he called Lisa. "Could I come by tomorrow evening?"

"Chuckie goes to bed at seven."

"Would six be too early?" he asked.

"I suppose not."

The next day he picked up Lisa's car at Logan's. "Looks great, Mac. How much?"

"For you, doc, fifty bucks, but don't be telling other folks the bargains you get."

"My lips are sealed, Mac." He winked.

It was just before six when he turned the car into Lisa's driveway. He rang the bell at the side door. When she came to the door, he pointed to her car. "Surprise!" He handed her the keys.

"Michael, you had it repaired."

"Just a few dents hammered out."

"You shouldn't have. It was Tom's responsibility."

He airily waved her objection aside. "Where's Chuckie?"

"In his highchair, just finishing his supper." She turned to the small figure, whose face was liberally smeared with applesauce. "Look who's here, Chuckie."

The little boy gave Michael a dazzling smile.

Lisa handed Shea a washcloth. "Give his face a swipe and take off his bib. I'll leave you two alone for a while. I have some errands to do."

As she backed the car out of the driveway, a look of annoyance crossed her face. It was nice of Michael to have the car fixed, but she hated being obligated to him. She drove on deep in thought. The Michael Shea she knew so well did nothing for anyone unless he thought there was something in it for him. Actually, she had no errands to do. She just wanted to get out of the house, away from Michael. One thing she had to admit, Michael adored Chuckie. She couldn't deny him the pleasure of seeing his son, and yet she found his weekly visits disturbing—and for good reason. Invariably he begged her to marry him. Just as invariably she refused. How long could this go on? It was a one-way street that led nowhere. She drove aimlessly.

Michael lifted his son from the highchair and hugged him. He carried him into the living room and stood before the mirror with the boy in his arms. Amazing how much they looked alike—the same bronze-reddish hair, the deep blue eyes, and when Chuckie smiled, it was Michael's smile.

He wanted down. They played games like Roll the ball and Where's Chuckie? Michael made paper airplanes and sailed them across the room. Chuckie retrieved them like an unreliable puppy. When he was tired, he brought a well-thumbed picture book to Michael and they "read" together.

Lisa returned a few minutes before seven and carried Chuckie upstairs to bed. While Michael waited for her to return, he thought, *One more chance. I'll give her one more chance. She seemed really pleased about the car. Maybe tonight she'll relent and say yes.*

She came into the living room. "Blue is your color," he told her, complimenting her on the dress she was wearing. "You never looked lovelier."

She ignored his comments. "The car never looked better. Thank you, Michael."

"Lisa, there's so much I want to do for you and Chuckie, so much I can do for the two of you. Things are going great for me at the hospital. Once more, Lisa, I'm asking you. Please say you'll marry me."

She shook her head. The memory came back, the chilling memory, of when she had put pride aside and, pregnant with their baby, had begged him to divorce Claire and marry her. His "No chance, Lisa" had been cold and firm. Well, there was no chance for him now. "Good night, Michael."

He gave her a strange smile. "I'll be back soon," he said and left.

As soon as he returned to his apartment, he dialed

the phone. Tom Hughes answered as he had hoped. "Hi, Tom. Dr. Shea here. How are you feeling?"

"Much better, thank you."

"I think I'd better have a look at those stitches early next week. Could you come in on Monday about three? And by the way, Tom, your mother has the car back good as new. You're welcome, Tom. Everything is delivered as promised. See you then Monday at three."

He replaced the receiver and leaned back in his chair. On Monday at three, he would have an announcement for Thomas Miller Hughes that should rock him a bit.

There was one more thing he must do before seeing Lisa again tomorrow. Might as well get it over with. He looked at his watch. Nine o'clock. If he drove directly to the Domino Club, he would be there in plenty of time for the floor show at ten. Then he would visit Lorraine in her dressing room and break the news. For just a moment he was tempted not to tell Lorraine. He shook his head. It was too risky in a town as close-knit as Oakdale to continue seeing her. There must be nothing that could jeopardize the outcome of his plan in any way. There was no place for Lorraine in the future he visualized.

The Domino Club was one of the notorious dives clustered around Oakdale. Located on the strip just outside the city limits, it was wide open and immune from any of the town's restrictions. A generous monthly gift to the county sheriff guaranteed no problems connected with operations in that area. For the most part, respectable citizens of Oakdale ignored the place, pretending it wasn't there. Its clientele was made up of the shadier Oakdale element, county swingers, and various visitors who were drawn to the gaming tables that operated upstairs. Shea had been a patron ever since coming to Oakdale. He was well known to the owners and on occasion had acted as the club's unofficial doctor. Every so often there was a fracas of some sort, and Shea would be called for medical aid. Once there had been an "accidental" shooting. He had removed a bullet lodged in one of the owner's shoulders and not seen fit to report it. The owner was most grateful.

He reached the Domino in good time for the ten o'clock floor show, was shown to his favorite table, and provided with his favorite drink. It wasn't much of a show, but the patrons didn't seem to mind. There was the inevitable comic who was more vulgar than funny, a dance team with delusions of Astaire and Rogers, and then the star of the show, Lorraine Durcel. She was obviously the crowd's favorite and certainly she was Michael Shea's favorite. Her songs were risqué, but delivered with a bewitching innocence. Underneath the artfully contrived innocence was a ruthless ego, as Shea well knew. It was this unscrupulous drive for success more than her pretty blonde looks that had attracted him. Their affair, with a few escapades on the side, had lasted for two years, something of a record for Michael Shea. As she finished her act, she spotted her lover and threw him a kiss. The goodbye kiss, Shea thought, although she doesn't know it. He made his way to her dressing room.

"What a surprise!" she said when he entered. "Where have you been and why didn't you return my calls?"

"I've been busy."

"Too busy for me?" She lit a cigarette. "Don't I get an apologetic kiss? A hug? A squeeze?"

He sat down. This wasn't going to be easy.

"Why so serious, Michael?" She affected a babyish pout. "What happened to the fun-loving Romeo I once knew?"

"Lorraine, I'm here to say goodbye."

"What do you mean?"

"I mean we have to stop seeing each other. I'm getting married."

She stubbed out her cigarette angrily. "Marriage never got in your way before!"

"This time is different. I'm marrying Chuckie's mother. I want no complications."

"So now I'm a complication!"

"Lorraine, it has to be this way. Nothing is going to endanger this marriage. Chuckie is going to have a father he can be proud of. We've had our fun, you and I. And now the party's over."

"I happen to love you, Michael."

He stood up. "Come off it, Lorraine. There's no need for a scene. You'll find love again." There was a note of sarcasm to his voice.

"I'm not giving you up, Michael!"

"Listen, babe," he said, his voice harsh, "there are a few sordid details about you that I know. If they got whispered around, your career would be over."

"I see," she said quietly.

"Goodbye, Lorraine."

"You'll be back, Michael," she told him as he closed the door. "You'll be back." It was as though she were making a promise to herself.

Shea called Lisa early Friday afternoon. "Lisa, I must see you this afternoon. It's important."

"It's Chuckie's nap time."

"I don't want to see Chuckie. I want to see you."

She detected the urgency in his voice. "Then come on over."

By the time he arrived, Chuckie was asleep. Shea sat on the divan facing Lisa and wasted no time getting to the point. "I'm determined that we get married and after I read this to you, I think you'll agree that we should." From his jacket pocket, he took out Tom's confession and read it without emotion to Lisa. He repeated the last sentence—"At the time of the theft I was fully conscious that such a crime was punishable by arrest and imprisonment if convicted."

He waited a minute. Lisa had paled. Her hands clutched the arms of the chair. "Unless you agree to marry me, Lisa, I'll take this to the police and press charges. It will probably ruin Tom's life. You can prevent this. My wedding present to you will be this signed confession, which you can then destroy."

Lisa spoke slowly. "Does Tom know that you're using his confession to force me to marry you?"

Michael shook his head. "He'll never know. When he signed it, I promised him that as long as he stayed off drugs, I wouldn't reveal his theft to the police."

Lisa's eyes widened, but she said nothing.

"I love you, Lisa. It can be a happy marriage. It will mean a new chance for Tom, and Chuckie has the right to have a father. You loved me once, Lisa. Remember?"

She bowed her head for a moment and then looked at him unwaveringly. "Very well, Michael. You win. We'll get married, but I warn you—if you don't keep your promises, I'll kill you."

He smiled smoothly. "You wouldn't kill Chuckie's father, now would you, Lisa?"

"I think you'd better go now, Michael." She was fighting for control.

"Very well, Lisa. I'll call you tonight and we'll discuss our wedding plans."

She nodded, too choked up to speak.

At the door he turned to her. "You've made a wise decision, Lisa."

On Monday Tom appeared as scheduled at Shea's office.

"Tom, you're looking much better." Michael Shea was his ingratiating self again, all smiles, all charm. "Sit down, Tom," he said. With something of a flourish, he unwound the bandage. "Coming along fine. We'll have the nurse fix you up with a smaller bandage, not quite so dramatic, before you leave."

Tom looked at him inquiringly.

"No problems, Tom. Everything has been arranged. Your record is clear."

"Thank you, Dr. Shea."

"And, Tom, congratulations are in order."

"Oh?"

"Your mother has finally agreed to marry me."

Tom's face registered disbelief.

Shea continued. "It'll be a quiet wedding. No fuss. No feathers. I think Lisa had her heart set on Valentine's Day, but I'm too impatient. We've set the date for a week from Wednesday."

"I hope you and Mother will be very happy, doctor."

"We will. We will. And you must call me Michael, now that I'll be part of the family. Shall we ring for the nurse?"

It was a small, early-evening parlor wedding. Lisa had suggested City Hall, but Michael would have none of it. There must be a few guests. He invited his nurse, who wept throughout the brief ceremony. Tom was there, and Lisa's mother, Alma Miller, who held a wide-eyed Chuckie on her lap. Lisa looked lovely and somewhat remote in a gray chiffon. Michael was quite dapper in his new tuxedo with satin lapels. A photographer friend of Michael's insisted on taking too many pictures.

The wedding cake had been baked by Alma Miller. There were the customary champagne toasts followed by cake and coffee. For a wedding party, it was a curiously quiet affair. Only Chuckie and Michael seemed excited. Alma had offered to take Chuckie home with her, but Lisa told her it wouldn't be necessary.

The few guests left as though on cue. Chuckie was put to bed. The kitchen help was paid and taken home by Michael. When he returned, Lisa was seated before the fireplace staring at the dying embers. He offered her a glass of champagne and sat down beside her. For a while they sipped in silence. The embers of the last log parted, and a shower of sparks disappeared up the chimney like spent fireworks.

Michael took Tom's signed confession from his pocket. "Shall I burn this for you?" he asked. She nodded, and he rose and threw it on the last of the embers. They watched the paper as it browned, then suddenly burst into flames.

"This marriage is going to work, Lisa," Michael said softly and put his arm around her waist, pressing her to him.

"Don't rush things, Michael." She pulled away from him and placed a hand against her forehead. "Too much champagne perhaps. I have a headache. Good night. I'm going to bed."

He sat alone. The fire was out. Very well, there would be other nights. The new husband would sleep in the guest room tonight. He switched off lights and slowly went up the stairs, stopping to look in on Chuckie. Carefully he removed the teddy bear from the bed and leaned over and gently kissed the sleeping child. He and his son were together under the same roof. He had won the first round of the game. He could afford to be patient with Lisa, but only for awhile.

Chapter Eight
Closed Doors

Oakdale's most elegant, most expensive boutique was Renée's. It was here that Lisa went shopping a few days after her marriage to Michael Shea. She was one of Renée's best customers, and when she entered the shop on a snowy Monday, the staff greeted her effusively. She accepted their best wishes for a long and happy marriage to Dr. Shea graciously. Sipping the coffee that had been brought to her, she asked to see the latest in lingerie. While she waited, she allowed herself to think about the past weekend. It had been difficult, and she frowned slightly as she recalled that in the game they seemed to be playing, she had come off distinctly second best.

On Saturday night she had let Michael push too many drinks on her. Understandably, he had mixed strong ones. It had been alcohol, not Michael, that had broken down her defenses. So she had submitted to his passion, and submitted was exactly the right word. She had lain in his arms and responded to his ardent lovemaking with all the fervor of a rag doll.

Even so, for the moment he was the victor and she the vanquished. But she hadn't given up. Before this she had not adequately outlined a strategy for herself in their marriage game. Now she had formulated a plan and she was eager to put it into action. Her thoughts were interrupted by Renée and an assistant. Instinctively they had decided what she wanted. The lingerie they showed her was seductive, to say the least—filmy, gossamer nightgowns, black, lacy panties with bras to match, negligee gauzy and translucent— that seemed to shimmer.

In the midst of this boudoir show, Susan Stewart entered the boutique. Lisa knew Dan Stewart's wife, of course. After all, everyone knew everyone in the Memorial Hospital social circle. Although they weren't close friends, they saw each other from time to time. Susan approached Lisa and gave her a congratulatory peck on the cheek. "So happy for you, my dear. You married quite an Irish charmer."

Lisa indicated the array of lingerie. "I know and I intend to do a little charming myself."

Susan Stewart held up a sheer peek-a-boo nightgown. She shivered. "I hope you don't catch your death of cold."

Lisa assumed a dreamy smile. "Our bedroom is quite warm, almost overheated."

Susan's laugh was light and brittle. "Well, enjoy the torrid zone while you can. I've discovered that doctors blow hot and cold."

Lisa looked sympathetic.

"As a matter of fact, I'm here to select a Las Vegas wardrobe," Susan announced.

"Oh! I didn't know—" Lisa began.

Susan cut in quickly. "Neither does Dan yet." She laughed without mirth. "I thought it would be wise to buy my traveling clothes before my accounts might be closed."

It was plain that Susan Stewart was angry, and although it was none of her concern, Lisa felt both embarrassment and sympathy—embarrassment that Susan had reached the point of reporting such private information to a casual friend, and in public at that. She also felt sympathy for a woman in such obvious distress.

"Why don't we finish our shopping here and then have lunch?" Susan suggested.

"I'd love that. I need someone to talk to."

They lunched at Roberto's. "I'm positive we won't run into Dan here," Susan said. "He loves Italian food, but he's trying to lose weight. He thinks it will help him to look young and handsome."

They ordered drinks, but it didn't take alcohol to loosen Susan's tongue. "On my way to Renée's I drove by the Wade Bookstore. It was just as I had expected."

Lisa looked puzzled.

"Dan's car was parked in front of the store. He's so busy buying books, I don't see how he finds time to be a doctor. God knows he finds no time to be a husband."

It was clear that Lisa's role was to be that of a listener. Still puzzled, she made small sympathetic sounds as Susan continued.

"Let's eat. Being angry always makes me hungry. That's why I've added a few pounds these last few months."

Their order given, Susan went on. "Now that his true love is available, I hate to play into his hands by getting a divorce, but the truth is I don't want him anymore. She can have him."

Suddenly Lisa realized who *she* was. Susan was

referring to Liz Stewart, the owner of Wade's Bookstore, available to Dan now that Paul Stewart was dead. *How many mixed-up lives there must be in Oakdale*, she thought, *including her own and Michael Shea's.* Now here was Susan complaining bitterly how Dan had neglected her.

"I'm buying a new lease on my life with the divorce," Susan said. "It's time I had some fun and kicked up my heels. How about tortoni for dessert?"

They parted with Susan promising to keep in touch with Lisa after the divorce. "Don't know where I'll be or what I'll do. The important thing is I'll be free!"

Susan waited up for Dan that night. When he returned home, it was late.

"Emergencies at the hospital," he explained. "Did you get the message I wouldn't be home for dinner?"

She nodded. "Sit down, Dan. I want to talk."

"Let me get a beer. I'm bushed." He was back soon with cheese and crackers and his beer.

Susan didn't mince words. "I'm getting a divorce, Dan."

He put down the beer and stared at her without comment.

"I'll be leaving for Las Vegas by the end of the week. I made an appointment for us to go to Chris Hughes's law offices tomorrow afternoon. Chris will handle this himself. After we've conferred with him, he'll get in touch with a Las Vegas lawyer he recommends."

"This is rather sudden, isn't it, Susan?"

"Sudden!" Her laugh was strident. "It's over five years now since you met Liz Talbot. Is that sudden? Four years since she had your baby and married Paul Stewart. Is that sudden? And since Paul died, it's started all over again with you and Liz. I won't be a neglected wife any longer, Dan."

He didn't argue, but he did ask, "What about the clinic? They need you there, Susan."

She looked at him angrily. "So typical of you, my dear, to be more interested in the clinic and the hospital than in me, as a human being. But to answer your heartfelt question, I'll simply take a leave of absence for the time being. But I can assure you we'll never work together again professionally. Never, ever!" She rose. "I'm hungry. I think I'll fix myself a sandwich and go to bed. Good night, Dan."

He sat there, drinking his beer. Amazing, he thought, that Susan would want a divorce now, after refusing him one when Liz was pregnant. The suddenness of her decision must have little to do with him or with Liz. There was something that Susan was holding back. Could it be that she had met someone else? It was quite possible. Susan was an attractive woman. True, she had put on some weight, and the flash and fire of youth might be gone, but she deserved better than she had received from him.

Strange that she hadn't even mentioned their daughter Emily. Motherhood was not Susan's strong point. She had handed Emily totally over to the excellent nurse who took care of her. Doubtless, Susan assumed such an arrangement would continue. This was something that must be discussed with Chris Hughes tomorrow. Life should not be disrupted for Emily. She should remain here in Oakdale under his roof with her faithful nurse.

There was little prospect of a custody battle, Susan versus Dan. Of that, he was almost certain. She did not want to be encumbered with a small child at this point. Never had, for that matter. Still they must reach a definite understanding tomorrow in front of Chris that he, Dan Stewart, was to have custody of

Emily. He looked at the clock. It was late, but not too late to call Liz. Surely Susan was asleep by now, but to be sure he wasn't overheard, he went to the den and used the private line. "Liz."

Her voice contained a note of surprise. "Dan? It's so late. Is something the matter?"

"I need to talk to you, Liz. May I come over for just a while?"

"Of course. You're all right?"

"I'm fine."

He left quietly, not that he really cared whether or not Susan heard him.

Liz was waiting. She had made a pot of tea. Liz and her tea, he thought fondly. Armed with it, she could face anything.

She looked so concerned. He took her in his arms and kissed her. "There's nothing to worry about."

They sat in the kitchen, and she placed a cup of tea for him on the table. "When I came home tonight, Susan told me that she was getting a Las Vegas divorce immediately."

She waited for him to go on.

"It means that we can get married if you'll have me."

"You know the answer to that," she said quietly.

He got up and stood beside her. "Nothing's going to spoil our chance for happiness now. I'll give Susan no cause to change her mind about the divorce. Good night, sweet Liz." He kissed her quickly and was gone.

Michael handed Lisa an ice-cold martini after she had settled herself on the divan before the fire. "You're looking very beautiful tonight, Mrs. Shea," he said.

She smiled. "You're a master of martinis. This is perfect."

"What did you do today?" he asked.

She decided not to destroy the ambience with an account of lunch with Susan and the news of the impending divorce. "Oh, just those things an expensive and dutiful wife does. A little shopping. A lot of time in the kitchen preparing a meal for the lord of the manor. If you're nice and say you like my cooking, I'll give you a fashion show after dinner."

Michael kissed her gently on the forehead. This was the Lisa he wanted, responsive, high-spirited, and provocative.

"And, Michael, the sled and the coasting today were inspirational. What a thrill for Chuckie! It takes a father to think of things like that."

Dinner was delicious. Lisa had done herself proud. He toasted her. "Your talents are many. And here's to one I never guessed—the queen of cuisine."

She was pleased. "Thank your mother-in-law," she told him. "She taught me everything I know."

They rinsed and stacked the dishes in the sink. "A surprise for Mrs. Fuller who starts tomorrow as chief cook and bottle washer," Lisa said gaily. "And now an after-dinner liqueur followed by a fashion show."

Michael put another log on the fire while they had their brandies. They talked of mundane things until Lisa, who had been thinking of Susan's disclosure, asked, "Is Dan Stewart well-liked at the hospital?"

"He's considered one of the best doctors there."

"But I asked if he's well-liked."

Michael looked at her quizzically. "Well, there are those who work with Susan—they think Dan has treated her shabbily. But why the sudden interest in Dan Stewart?"

She regretted bringing up the matter. "Oh, just some gossip I heard today that things weren't going well between him and Susan."

Michael laughed knowingly. "That's the understatement of the evening."

Lisa gazed into her brandy glass. "'Oh, what a tangled web we weave when first we practice to deceive.' My mother quoted that to me at least once a week when I was growing up." Suddenly her mood changed. "It's time for the fashion show. Wait here. I'll be back just as soon as I change costumes."

After she left the room, Michael reflected on her amazing turnaround. This new Lisa was a bit of a riddle. What next? he wondered.

"Tah dah, ta de de, tah dah!" Lisa announced her presence with a fanfare. He turned around. She was at the top of the stairs in a filmy red negligee that literally took his breath away. Slowly she came down the stairway as if it were a runway in a burlesque house, no bumps or grinds, but opening the dressing gown now and then to reveal a tantalizing expanse of leg and thigh. She swept into the room and stood between him and the fire, her lovely figure outlined, like a shadow play, by the glow from the fireplace.

"Second act," she murmured, and opened the negligee. She was wearing the briefest of black lacy panties with a matching bra.

He applauded and held out his arms to her.

The telephone rang.

It was the hospital calling. There was an emergency, a bad highway accident. Could he come in at once?

"What timing!" he remarked wryly, and gave Lisa a hurried kiss. "God knows when I'll be back."

"To be continued," Lisa said, with a slow, understanding smile. "Damn," she muttered under her breath as he closed the door. So her plan was aborted for the moment, just when things had been going exactly as she had visualized. She stared at the dying fire and sighed. Well, she would have to set the stage again tomorrow night.

It was four in the morning when Michael returned. Quietly he got ready for bed and then went down the hall to Lisa's room. Her door was locked. He shrugged and retraced his steps. "To be continued," he repeated to himself and smiled.

As arranged, Mrs. Fuller arrived at nine the next morning. Lisa was waiting with instructions. She explained to Mrs. Fuller that Michael had had an emergency call and would be sleeping late. "Please tell him that I have taken Chuckie and gone to see my mother."

The drive to Rockford was pleasant and short enough so that Chuckie didn't get restless. Alma Miller had moved to Rockford from the farm shortly after Lisa's father died. An independent woman, strong-willed, she had found a small cottage within walking distance of a shopping mall. She lived alone. Cooking was her greatest pleasure and she supplemented her modest income, which inflation was beginning to shrink, by baking bread, pies, cakes, and cookies. She had a host of satisfied, eager customers. The house always smelled of spices, chocolate, and fresh homemade bread.

Alma Miller was expecting them. Indeed she had invited them. There were things she needed to talk over with Lisa.

But first there were cookies and milk for Chuckie and a visit to the closed-in back porch to see the new kittens that Feisty, Alma's favorite cat, had presented her with. Lisa sat in the kitchen while her mother iced a couple of cakes. They had a light lunch at the kitchen table, and then Chuckie was persuaded to take his nap early so that he could "try out" the new quilt that Alma had just finished for him.

It was good to sit and rest a bit. Lisa looked at her mother. She was hemming some tea-towels, but after a moment, she stopped and looked directly at Lisa. "I saw Dr. Perry last week," she announced.

"Oh!"

"He says I must slow down. My blood pressure is up, and he claims I'm anemic."

"Then you must do what the doctor ordered," Lisa said.

"I told him I wasn't about to give up my cooking or my sewing, and he said, 'Then get yourself some help, Alma. You shouldn't be living alone, anyway.'" She paused.

Lisa decided to call Dr. Perry as soon as she returned home. She had a feeling that her mother wasn't telling the complete story.

Unexpectedly, her mother admitted she thought the doctor was right. "It would be nice to have someone around to lean on a little. Sometimes I get lonely. I called Cousin Annie, who just has a room at Mrs. Stone's boarding house. She's going to move in with me. Annie's neat as a pin and she won't get in the way."

As usual her mother had faced the problem, taken charge, and solved it. Lisa knew better than to offer her financial help for the added expense that Annie's living with her would mean. But she knew Annie. Through her, Lisa could help, and Annie would be discreet.

"I'm delighted that Annie's going to be with you. She's good company."

Her mother raised her eyebrows but didn't challenge the statement. "Anyway I hope we like the same TV shows." She shot a quick look at Lisa. "You and

Michael happy?" The eyebrows stayed raised.

Lisa wasn't about to worry her mother with their marital problems, but she knew also that she couldn't get by with a glowing account of a situation that didn't exist. "We're working at it," she said.

Chuckie and Lisa were home by four o'clock and she immediately put in a call to Dr. Perry. He listened while she told him what her mother had said. "I would have called you, Lisa, but she told me not to, that you had problems enough of your own right now."

How had her mother known? She reads minds, Lisa decided. "Then she didn't tell me everything?" Lisa asked.

The doctor's voice was calm, but not reassuring. "Your mother has leukemia, Lisa."

The word chilled her, but before she could question him, the doctor continued. "There's no cause for immediate alarm. With the treatment I've prescribed and her own determination and common sense, we should arrest this condition for some time." He told Lisa more of what to expect.

"One thing, doctor," Lisa said before she hung up, "Mother's independence is very important to her, but she does worry about finances. Send her a modest bill each month, and bill me for the remainder."

He agreed. "You may want to check with the pharmacy, too," he said. "The medication will be expensive."

So, Lisa thought, *I'll postpone tonight's performance for Michael. When he comes home, I'll tell him about Mother, explain that it's been a traumatic day for me, ask him for a sleeping pill, and go to bed. He'll understand.*

Indeed, he did, insisting on tucking her in himself. "You're my most special patient," he told her and brought her water and a couple of pills. "Take these and you'll be asleep in no time." Gently he kissed her good night. "I'll call Dr. Perry myself and talk to him about your mother. Everything that can be done will be done, believe me."

She lay there in the dark, trying to piece together the happenings of the day into some semblance of reality. As she drifted towards a dreamless sleep, she thought, Michael can be kind. He can be.

Downstairs Michael Shea poured himself a drink and stood before the window. It was snowing again, a slow but persistent snow. There was a comforting look to it, which he realized was deceptive. It was the kind of snow that weighed down branches until they broke, the kind of snow that could pick up momentum until its cold fury could paralyze. How long could he be slow and comforting and patient? he wondered. How long?

The next day, Susan Stewart called Lisa from Chicago. Because of the weather, her Las Vegas flight had been delayed. "I wanted to get in touch with Chris Hughes," she said. "This weather has caused all sorts of problems. I can't reach him. Would you see if you can locate Chris and tell him to call me here at the Blackstone?"

"Of course, I will, Susan. Is it still snowing there?"

"A blizzard. Don't know when I'll get out."

Then quite distinctly at Susan's end of the line, Lisa heard a masculine voice say, "Susan, where's the toothpaste?"

There was a pause and then Susan said, sounding flurried, "Have to go, Lisa. Room service just arrived."

As she hung up the phone, Lisa smiled. Interesting room service, she reflected, that calls a hotel guest by her first name. Obviously, Susan was not alone in Chicago. There was a strong possibility that her bid for a divorce had been caused by more than Dan's interest in Liz. Quite possibly Susan had an interest of her own.

Dan and Liz, and now Susan and someone! What a romantic rigmarole, Lisa thought. Change partners and dance!

It was time again to focus on her relationship with Michael. Perhaps tonight would be the time to restage the interrupted fashion show.

Chapter Nine
Flight

Once again Lisa was forced to postpone the fashion show for Michael. She and Chuckie were snowed in. At three in the afternoon, Michael called from the hospital to say that the staff was on call until the snow emergency was over. Weather predictions were for at least another twelve hours of snow. Most roads were impassable.

Were she and Chuckie all right? "Snug as bugs in a rug," Lisa told him, "and Mrs. Fuller is spending the night with us. We've plenty of provisions and there are no wolves at the door as far as I know." She sounded happy and excited.

They retired early. One lamp turned low, and the fire from the fireplace provided enough light. Mrs. Fuller was soon asleep. Lisa lay on the divan. The wind was dying down. It sighed restlessly through the pines, singing a wintry lament. Home was once more a haven. Strange that she should find this curious comfort. It was a welcome respite. Stormy outside though it was, this was a lull before the personal storm that was brewing for her to face. It was good to relax even temporarily. She slept.

The distant hum of the furnace and the whirr of the kitchen refrigerator woke her up. The fire was out in the fireplace, but its warmth still lingered. Even so, it was reassuring to know that the furnace was at work again. The sky was gray, but not threatening. A few snowflakes drifted down listlessly. The world outside was white and silent and undisturbed as yet.

Mrs. Fuller and Chuckie were still sleeping. Lisa blew out the lamp and quietly padded out to the kitchen to make Chuckie's oatmeal. And wasn't it good to know that the coffee maker would perk and that the juicer would produce orange juice?

She was back in the world of reality. Home was no longer a haven. It was a game board, and tonight, without fail, she would continue the marriage game.

Michael was home from the hospital shortly after noon. Dead tired, he showered and then prepared to take a nap. "Wake me up in time to go to bed," he told her.

It was seven o'clock when he awakened. They had a drink, and he recounted some of the problems the storm had created for the hospital staff. There were always some people who didn't have sense enough to stay in when it stormed. So there had been accidents, and more than the usual number of pregnant women who decided the baby was on its way. One of the ambulances had become stuck in a drift and put out of commission, and believe it or not, there had been three emergency appendectomies. It had been a rough night for all concerned.

They had a bowl of Mrs. Fuller's vegetable soup and retreated to the living room.

"How about a continuation of the fashion show?"

Lisa's voice and glance were provocative.

"Just the thing for a weary doctor," he responded.

Once again she disappeared.

He didn't intend to, but waiting for her, he dozed off. When he opened his eyes, she was standing before him. This time the negligee was blue, his favorite color for her. Slowly, she opened the gauzy dressing gown. Underneath it was the sheerest of nightgowns. It was more like a veil than a nightgown, revealing her beautiful body with all its allure.

"One moment, sir," she said and walked over to the record player. In a moment, she was dancing before him to the strains of "I'm in the Mood for Love," swaying, turning, closer and closer, but always just out of reach. Then the record changed, and to the lilt of "Come to Me, Bend to Me," she was dancing again. Nearer and nearer she came, her lips parted in a beckoning smile. He was no longer the weary doctor.

"Lisa, Lisa," he said. "Come to me!"

But she danced away from him, on and on, until she reached the foot of the stairs. The record player clicked off. He got up and walked toward her, ardent, filled with yearning.

She moved, always a step ahead of him, to the head of the stairs. For a moment she paused. Standing there in the soft light of the hallway, her negligee fully open to reveal her soft, rounded body, she had never seemed so enticing, so tantalizing. And then quickly she moved down the hall and entered her room. The door closed behind her. He heard the key turn in the lock.

"Lisa!"

Through the door he heard a low laugh.

"What is this? Some sort of game?" he asked.

There was no answer.

"Damn it, Lisa! This isn't funny." He put his ear to

the door. Was she there just inside, teasing him with this witchery, preparing at the last moment to open the door and herself to him?

"Lisa, please." He waited and listened. There was a long silence, and then Lisa's voice, cool, remote, and final: "Good night, Michael."

So this was how it was to be! He thought of Lorraine and the Domino Club, and with difficulty pushed that out of his mind. No! He was not giving up. He would play the waiting game, but only for a while. In the end he would win—he was confident of that. *I am smarter than Lisa and stronger, and let's admit it*, he told himself, *I'm more of a schemer*. Also there was Chuckie. Michael lay on his bed and thought of ways he could use Chuckie as a means to gain what was rightfully his.

During the next week, Michael made no overt moves. Lisa discontinued her fashion show. They observed the niceties. Lisa usually went to bed early. Sometimes after putting Chuckie to bed, she didn't come back downstairs at all.

Michael spent more time at the hospital. To add to his problems, he was receiving daily notes from Lorraine. They were addressed to the hospital and marked *Personal*.

It was a strange dilemma, Michael reflected. The woman he wanted didn't want him. The woman he no longer wanted insisted that he return. Something had to be done about Lorraine, but for once he was at a loss. He began returning her letters unopened. If that didn't work, he would think of something else, but he would wait and see. Meanwhile there was Lisa, so beautiful, so near, so infuriatingly remote. His patience was wearing thin.

It was now nearly two weeks since Lisa had

deliberately inflamed his desire for her and then mocked him from the other side of her locked bedroom door. At dinner, they generally made polite conversation, mainly for Mrs. Fuller's benefit. Now they sat across from each other in the living room, Lisa engrossed in a book, Michael watching television with little interest. He got up and turned off the set. She looked up from her novel. "Lisa," he said, "this has gone too far. Please come to bed with me. Let me show you how wonderful love can be."

She gave him a look of pity and disgust. Then she got up, taking her book with her, and walked toward the stairs. In an instant he caught up with her. His hands dug into her shoulders. "Don't make me use force, Lisa."

She turned and hit him on the side of the head with her book. The blow was ineffective, but it startled him. She pulled away from his grasp and ran up the stairs. By the time he reached her bedroom, the door was once again closed and locked. He pounded on it. "Lisa!"

She spoke to him through the door. "Hush! You'll wake up Chuckie. Do you really want to frighten your son?"

He turned abruptly and walked away. It was as though they had declared war, and Chuckie was to be the weapon.

The following days and nights were extremely difficult for both of them, but most of all for Lisa. She lived in fear. Michael could resort to force, and the idea of physical violence was appalling. Should she succumb and submit to him to preserve a marriage based on a threat in the beginning? Could Chuckie grow up normally, cared for but a pawn between a mother and father at bitter odds with each other?

Desperately, she wished for someone—a friend, anyone—to talk to, to confide in.

It was unfair to involve Tom in this situation, a situation, which in part, he had brought about. He must never know that his confession had been the cause of her accepting marriage with Michael. Yet it would be a good thing to talk with Tom, to find out how he was getting along, to show him how interested she was in what he was doing. It would help take her mind off her own troubles. She would invent some reason for him to come over—have some gifts for him for some reason. Michael had told her that Tom was looking for a job. Reason enough! She decided to make a quick trip to Wade's Bookstore.

At the bookstore, Lisa looked for gifts for Tom. She had already decided on an appointment book and an address pad as something a job-hunter would find useful. And while he waited for interviews, as one always waited and waited, a good book to pass away those restless moments would be a godsend.

Liz Stewart came forward to wait on her. She recognized Lisa as Michael Shea's wife. They had met at a recent hospital benefit. Liz had gone there with Dan. There had been some snide looks and cool greetings, but Lisa had been warm and friendly. "Mrs. Shea, may I help you?" Liz asked her now.

They discussed books that Tom would enjoy. Liz was a good salesperson; in addition to the address and appointment books, Lisa bought three novels, two for Tom and one for herself. On the drive home Lisa found herself thinking of Liz Stewart. How bright and clever she was, and how extraordinarily happy she looked, as though it were the best of all possible worlds. Lisa felt envious.

At home she put in a call to Tom. Could he come by

for lunch the following day? She had something for him. He was surprised and grateful. He had been afraid that she was angry with him for wrecking her car. He would be there at one o'clock.

Lisa took special pains with the lunch. Mrs. Fuller could feed Chuckie and start preparations for the evening meal, but she would cook for Tom. Something hearty for a growing boy and not too fancy. She prepared a ham and with it a pot of beans baked slowly to perfection. Potato chips, of course. Everyone had a right to a certain amount of junk food. And for dessert, a chocolate pie.

It was a delicious lunch, and, yes, Tom was job-hunting. Dr. Shea had given him some leads which he appreciated.

"And how's your father?" she asked and suddenly, unexpectedly, she felt a surge of emotion as she thought of Bob Hughes, level-headed, practical Bob. He could give her words of advice that would be helpful. She would never talk to him, of course. It would be totally inappropriate and uncalled for, and yet . . .

"Dad's fine," Tom was saying. "He works too hard. I wish I saw more of him."

Why wouldn't it be all right to call Bob soon and suggest that he try to spend more time with their son? She should too, she reminded herself. Tom needed their support.

She gave him the gifts.

"But why? It isn't Christmas or my birthday even."

She remembered all the Christmases and birthdays that she had missed spending with him, but she said, "Because a job-hunter needs all the help he can get." She produced a box of neckties. "You really must wear a tie when you go for an interview, Tom. And don't wear jeans or sneakers," she advised.

He almost said, "You sound like a mother," and then realized that she had every right. He looked at this woman, his mother, who had came back into his life after so many years. She was still beautiful, but her face was drawn. There were worry lines he had not seen before, and dark circles under her eyes. Her voice was too brittle, and her animation served only to cloak a nervousness. He wanted to say, "What's wrong, Mom? What's bothering you?" but they had not reached that stage in their relationship. He thanked her for the gifts and for lunch and went on his way.

That night when Bob Hughes came home, Tom was waiting for him. "Had lunch with Mom today," he told his father casually and went on to tell him of the gifts.

"Nice of her," Bob Hughes said with no show of interest.

"Dad, it's none of your business, I know, but there's something worrying Mom. It was nothing she said to me, but I could tell by the way she looked. She chain-smoked. Something is wrong."

Bob looked at his son—this sensitive, insecure boy who was trying so hard to straighten out his own life. And now he was worrying about his mother. If his mother had worried about him many years ago, things might not have become so difficult for Tom now. Go easy, Bob told himself. Whatever the problem, if there indeed is a problem, Tom must not get involved.

"I'm sorry," he said, "but don't worry." Maybe I should speak to Shea, he thought. If it's something physical, he could suggest to Lisa that she have a checkup. He paused. "I know that your grandmother Miller isn't well. Shea mentioned it to me. That's probably what's worrying your mother."

Tom looked relieved. "Good night, Dad."

After he left, Bob eased himself into his favorite chair and sighed. Tom was so young, he reflected. He thinks there must be an answer to every question, a solution for every problem. What's more, Bob hadn't even had the chance to tell Tom of the good news. Well, that could wait. It was some time ahead. But to be chosen as one of the country's outstanding cardiologists to attend an international conference in Switzerland was an honor, and a well-deserved one, he told himself, as he recalled the long hours at Memorial, his studies, his research. He had buried his own problems with an overload of work, but it had paid off. He felt a little sheepish at being in such a self-congratulatory mood, but life, if not personally satisfying, was exciting professionally. His thoughts were interrupted by the insistent ringing of the telephone.

"Bob?"

"Yes."

"This is Lisa. Sorry it's late, but I wanted to talk with you. Is Tom around?"

"Gone to bed. He told me that he had a nice lunch with you."

"Oh, well—yes. Bob, I think he needs to see more of you, and I should give him more time too."

"I agree, Lisa. How are you? And how's Michael?" It was difficult to bridge the years with mundane questions.

"Michael?" A steel trap could not have cut off the two syllables of the name more decisively. "Late at the hospital, as usual."

Suddenly her voice changed. It was warmer, more Lisa-of-the-old-times. "Bob, could I see you? Maybe lunch someplace? I need to talk to you."

They arranged to meet the next day at a busy hotel dining room that no one could conceivably consider a rendezvous. Several meetings followed. Bob soon realized that he was a listening post. There was nothing he could do but be sympathetic. The violence brewing between Lisa and Michael was obvious. He was worried.

The showdown night was bound to come, and it did on a windy, rainy night in mid-March. Michael lurched in about nine o'clock. He was drunk, unusual for him, and Lisa sensed immediately that to avoid any problems, she should go to her room. He barred the way. "God damn it, Lisa, I'm going to have you tonight. On the floor if necessary."

She kicked him in the groin and he doubled over with pain. "You bitch," he finally managed to say.

She tried to move past him.

"Listen to me," he said. "I'll never try to touch you again. You are all bitches, all of you."

There was no way that Lisa could know that he was also including Lorraine in that category. He had tried to reason with Lorraine at the Domino Club before coming home. It had been a searing scene, ending when Lorraine said in words that had the weight of steel, "You can't throw Lorraine Durcel aside like a has-been. If I can't have you, Michael Shea, then nobody will have you." There was nothing to say to that but to slam the door and leave.

And here he was with his dearest enemy. Well, he had a statement or two for her. "You can't outsmart me, Lisa. I've had you tailed for the last couple of weeks. All your sweet little rendezvous with Bob Hughes are documented. With your past performances also on record, I can go to court and prove without a doubt that you're an unfit mother for Chuckie, just as you were unfit as a mother for Tom. And I will, Lisa, I will. You're no good. Bad news for everyone. You'll get rid of me, all right, but you'll lose Chuckie in the bargain. I'll win custody. No doubt about that."

She flinched as though he had struck her.

Late the next morning after Lisa had carefully made her plans, she called her travel agent. They, Chuckie and she, were going to Mexico City, she explained. Chuckie had a persistent cold that a change of climate might rectify. Could the agent make immediate reservations, hotel and airline, and call her back? The travel agent obliged and within the next hour, Lisa was on the phone with Annie. "How's Mother?"

"Well enough," responded Annie in the guarded voice one uses when she is being overheard.

Lisa gave the number in Mexico City where she could be reached. No, she didn't know how long she would be there. "I'll keep in touch," she said. "And, Annie, if Dr. Shea calls, you haven't heard from me."

"I understand, ma'am," Annie assured her.

With Mrs. Fuller she had to be more factual. "Dr. Shea and I are parting, at least for the time being. I'm taking Chuckie." She paused and smiled faintly. "We're headed for destinations unknown. You can tell him, if he asks, that it will be useless to try to trace us. Here's a month's pay in advance. If he wants you to stay on, that's fine. The month's pay is yours. You've been a gem."

By three o'clock, Lisa and Chuckie were on their way to Chicago. She had arranged a night flight from Chicago to St. Louis to make it more difficult for Michael to follow them. They made connections and by mid-evening she checked into a hotel in St. Louis.

The flight to Mexico City was scheduled for the next morning at ten-thirty.

Once Chuckie was asleep, it occurred to her that she should inform Tom where she would be. She knew that Bob was on his way to the conference in Switzerland by this time. She placed the call and Tom answered. She must be careful, say nothing that would over-excite him. Play it cool, she told herself.

"This is your mother, Tom. I'm on my way to Mexico."

His voice was disbelieving. "Where are you, Mom?"

Better not tell. Tom would be one of the first people Michael would call.

"Oh, Kansas City, I think. Yes, Kansas City."

"Mom, are you all right?"

His voice, so warm with concern, was suddenly too much for her. She started crying.

"Mom! Mom! What's the matter?"

"I'm being silly, Tom," she said between sobs. "Things haven't been going well with Michael and me. Chuckie and I are taking a little vacation. We'll be back when things are straightened out."

"Mom, what can I do? How can I help?"

"Check on your grandmother now and then. Go see her if you can find the time. I'll send you my address later."

"Sure. Sure."

"And, Tom, if Michael calls you, don't tell him where I am. It's very important that he doesn't come after Chuckie and me."

Tom sensed the fear and the panic in her voice. "I promise, Mom."

"Good night, Tom. I love you."

He stared at the telephone after the call was completed. She had called him, he reflected. His mother had turned to him. For the moment they were apart, but now they were truly reunited. When she had said, "I love you, Tom," the words had taken on a new meaning. There was nothing he wouldn't do for her.

The phone rang again.

"Tom?" It was Michael Shea. "Have you heard from your mother?"

"Not recently."

"You're lying, Tom. Your line was just busy. Where is she?"

"I don't know, Dr. Shea. Don't you know?"

"You know damn well she's left me and taken Chuckie. I can tell by your voice. I intend to find them, Tom. I'll be by your place in the morning to take you to the office. There's something I want to show you that may refresh your memory. Just possibly you'll remember where your mother is, after all."

Chapter Ten

Encounters

After Michael Shea called Tom, he mixed himself a drink and sat down to plan a course of action. First he must find out where Lisa and Chuckie were. Tom certainly must know, and with a threat or two he could pry the information out of him. Once he knew where Lisa was, he could pressure her into coming back.

She had been a fool to think he would burn Tom's signed confession. The original was still in his office safe. She hadn't even asked to look at the copy he had so carefully prepared. He could have thrown a blank sheet of paper in the fireplace that night and she wouldn't have known the difference. The signed confession could be used again, and he planned to use it.

The telephone startled Michael. It was so late. Maybe Lisa had had second thoughts about leaving him. Maybe something had happened to Chuckie. He rushed to answer it.

It was Lorraine. Instantly it occurred to Michael

that she had learned that Lisa had left him. Impossible, he thought.

"Michael, it's between shows. Please come over. We must talk."

"Damn it, Lorraine! I told you never to call here."

"I know Lisa isn't at home. How could it matter?"

He was caught off-guard. "How did you know?"

Actually she had talked to Mrs. Fuller earlier. The housekeeper had been discreet, but had informed her that Mrs. Shea and Chuckie were out of town. "I have my sources, Michael," Lorraine said, with a hint of mystery in her voice.

He wondered how much she knew. "I'm not coming over, Lorraine. Now or ever."

"Then I'm coming over to your place. I'll grab a cab."

He was furious. "Lorraine, if you come over, I won't let you in. Can't you get it through your thick skull that we're through, kaput, fini? Goodbye."

"Don't you dare hang up on me."

"Listen, you little tramp, one move out of you and I'll tell your bosses about your Chicago connections with their rivals, and some of the deals you've pulled."

There was silence at the other end of the line—and then, "Two can play that game, Michael. I can smear your name all over the front pages too."

Michael laughed. "Nobody would believe a two-bit tramp like you. Get lost, Lorraine." He slammed down the receiver.

For an hour or so, he waited in the dark, having another drink and then another to calm his jangled nerves. No cab appeared. Lorraine had evidently come to her senses. He stumbled into bed.

Michael Shea wasn't a practiced drinker. When he woke up the next morning, he felt distinctly hungover. Even after some medication and a try at breakfast, he still was under the weather. But it was imperative that he see Tom Hughes. He called and told Tom he would be by for him within the hour.

There was little conversation between them on the way to Shea's office. Michael managed a couple of trivial questions. Had Tom followed any of the job leads he'd given him? The answer was that he had had a couple of interviews, but nothing definite yet. Was his father enjoying the medical conference in Switzerland? Tom had heard from Bob a few days before. "It's a very interesting conference, and he's accepted an invitation for a series of lectures in some medical school in Vienna. He'll be gone for over a month."

Tom looked at his watch. Lisa and Chuckie must be on their way. She had mentioned a ten-thirty flight.

Tom was right. Lisa and Chuckie had checked out of their hotel and were en route to the airport. It was a good day for flying—clear sky, calm weather. Lisa was confident that she had made the right decision. She and Chuckie could not and would not remain in exile forever, but this would give her time to concentrate on the future. Once she was settled, she would find a lawyer and explore the possibilities of a Mexican divorce.

Surely there was someone in Mexico City she knew. At the airport she rummaged through her purse for her address book. Joan and Lester Coleman, of course. She had known them when she'd lived in Chicago. For the last few years, they had gone to Mexico City to spend the winter. She would call them. They could be very helpful.

All at once she was aware that Chuckie was no longer by her side. Only a minute before, he had been looking at his picture book. Momentarily she panicked. The thought flashed through her mind that somehow Michael had followed them and snatched Chuckie away in the brief time she had been searching for her address book. Impossible, of course, but where had Chuckie gone? Little ones could be so quick— they could slip away so fast and silently. And Chuckie had just learned the game of hide-and-seek and loved to play it. "Chuckie!" she called, and looked for him in the row of seats just behind her. He was not there. "Chuckie," she called more loudly this time. Where could he be? She left her luggage and walked to the center aisle.

And then she saw him. He was standing by a glass case of toys just across the way, but how could he have gone so far, so quickly? A man was talking to him, and Chuckie was pointing excitedly at something in the toy case. She joined them.

"Chuckie," she said, "you should have told Mommy what you wanted." She was aware of the extraordinarily handsome man by her side, silver-haired, but with a youthful, deeply tanned face, and brown eyes that seemed to twinkle. "I'm sorry," she told him. "He got away so quickly."

"Don't blame him," the man said. "I think that teddy bear is to blame."

Chuckie was pointing at a small teddy bear behind the glass. He was almost crooning to it.

"It's very much like one he has at home. We forgot to bring it." She called to the clerk. "I'd like to buy the little teddy bear with the red jacket." She handed her a fifty-dollar bill.

"I can't change that, ma'am."

Lisa fumbled through her wallet for something smaller, but couldn't find it. She was flustered. The bills all seemed to stick together.

They were calling her flight. "Chuckie, there's no time. We'll find you a teddy bear in Mexico City, I promise."

He started to cry.

"Please let me," the man said. He produced a ten-dollar bill.

"Oh, no."

"You can reimburse me later. It seems we're on the same flight. Mexico City?"

She nodded.

He handed the teddy bear to Chuckie. "My name is Jay Watson."

"Mrs. Michael Shea," Lisa said. "And thank you."

When she collected her carry-on luggage, he was at her side. "Let me help you," he said. As they walked to the departure area, he made conversation. "I've been in St. Louis on business and now I'm returning to Mexico City. Do you live there?"

"First time there," Lisa said.

"It's an exciting city." He smiled. "I'd love to show you some of my favorite places."

He's a fast worker, Lisa thought, but she was pleased. It boosted her ego to be reminded that she was still attractive enough to elicit such a response. Maybe she wouldn't need to call the Colemans, after all. Anyway, the long trip to Mexico City was not going to be as boring as she had feared. And it was comforting to have such a good-looking, dependable man so eager to be of assistance. She returned his smile. "That's very kind of you."

Lisa would not have been smiling if she knew what was happening in Michael Shea's office at that moment. When he arrived at Memorial Hospital,

Michael immediately ushered Tom into his private office and closed the door. "Sit down, Tom." Michael's unsmiling face was like a mask. His eyes bore into Tom. "Now tell me where your mother is. No stalling, Tom."

Tom looked at him evenly. "I don't know, Dr. Shea." There was contempt in his voice. "I told you last night that I didn't know. I don't know this morning any more than I knew last night."

"And you won't know tomorrow or the next day or the next, if I'm the one asking, will you, Tom?"

The boy simply stared at him. "Why did Mother leave you, Dr. Shea?"

Michael ignored the question and walked over to his safe. Slowly, deliberately, he held out Tom's written confession which he had removed from the safe. His manner was cold and confident. "The police would still be very interested in this, Tom. Where are Lisa and Chuckie?"

"Why did Mother leave you, Dr. Shea?"

Shea's forehead throbbed with pain. Tom's manner was maddening. He wanted to grab the boy by the throat.

"How come you're so loyal to Lisa? She deserted you when you needed her. Left you behind when you were a baby and ran away to Chicago. She's been a poor excuse for a mother."

Tom's face whitened. "Why did she leave you, Dr. Shea?"

Shea's anger exploded. "She left me because I was ready to prove she was an unfit mother for Chuckie, just as she was an unfit mother for you. She was afraid she would lose Chuckie. My Chuckie!"

Tom stared at him. "Why in the hell did she marry you, Dr. Shea?"

Shea shook Tom's confession in his face.

The boy continued quietly. "Why in the hell would she marry a conniving bastard like you? I just can't understand it."

Once again Shea held out the confession.

Tom brushed it aside like an annoying fly. "My mother has made some mistakes, most of them understandable. But you're the worst mistake she ever made. How did you force her to marry you, Dr. Shea?" He sat there waiting for an answer.

With a great effort at control, Shea spoke to Tom. The words came out almost as though someone were strangling him. "You—you're as big an idiot as your mother." He pointed to the confession he held. "With this, you fool. I took your confession to your mother and told her I would go to the police if she refused to marry me." He paused for breath. "I—I told her that she'd be responsible for ruining your life—if she didn't marry me."

Tom got up from his chair.

"It was so easy!" Shea was more in control, speaking more easily, with an air of triumph as he recalled the scene. "I promised to burn your confession after she and I were married." He laughed. "And I did! I did! While she watched, I threw it in the fireplace. Only it was just a copy, just a copy. She never even asked to look at it, dummy that she is."

Tom retreated a step, as though Shea's words were blows pushing him, forcing him backward.

Once more Shea waved the confession at him. "And I'm ready to use this again, you son-of-a-bitch, if you don't tell me where Lisa is." He pointed at Tom. "And when I give this to the police and you're arrested, that will bring Lisa out of hiding, too. She'll come running to see if she can help her little darling in some way. I can't lose. Don't you see—I can't lose!"

There was no immediate response from Tom. They stood facing each other. Shea's face, mottled by his rage and his triumph, seemed enlarged to Tom, hanging suspended like a malicious, evil genie. Tom had become quite pale and he was still immobile. For an instant there was only silence punctuated by Shea's labored breathing. It was as though they were in a vacuum or the eye of a hurricane.

Then, with the fury of that hurricane, the young man hurled himself at Shea. No words. All his energy, all his strength, his youth, and his suddenly unleashed anger went into pounding, pounding this miserable, despicable excuse for a human being. The blows landed relentlessly on Shea's terror-stricken face, on his head. He tried to call out for help, but Tom's fist, square in his mouth, rendered him speechless. Blood gushed from his nose. Then after one final right to the chin, Michael Shea toppled, falling backward like a statue of stone, his head striking the corner of his desk.

Tom stood over him in a daze, scarcely seeing the crumpled figure on the floor. He shook his head as though he were in doubt that any of this could have happened. If the mist would clear, he would be alone, at home, anywhere but here. He bent over Michael Shea. There was no sign of life that he could detect. With a shudder, he turned away and then deliberately, he forced himself to look again at his victim. Michael Shea's right hand still clutched the signed confession. Tom reached out and unclenched the stiff fingers. The confession was his. He wadded it into a ball and shoved it into his pocket.

Then he let himself out of the office. There was no need for caution; the corridor was quite deserted. He walked as if in a dream or a nightmare down the hall, out into the open. As he walked, for the moment aimlessly, he took the crumpled ball of paper from his pocket and smoothed it out. His eyes focused only on his signature, Thomas Miller Hughes. With an effort he fished a book of matches from his jacket pocket. There on the street, in the bitter cold, he burned the paper and ground the ashes into dust with his heel. It was so strange, as though he were in an alien world. Nothing was recognizable. At that moment, he didn't have the slightest idea where he was. A cab came down the street, and he hailed it.

"Where to, buddy?"

"Take me to the police station," he told the driver.

At the police station, he said to the officer on the desk in a flat, unemotional tone, "I'm here to turn myself in. I just killed a man."

The police sergeant was incredulous. What was this nicely dressed, clear-eyed, clean-cut kid saying?

"Just a minute," he said. "You on the level?"

Tom nodded.

The police sergeant collected himself. "You need a lawyer. You got one?"

Tom found it difficult to concentrate, but finally he said, "My grandfather, Chris Hughes."

The sergeant's eyes widened. Chris Hughes? The town patriarch. This was no run-of-the-mill encounter.

"I think you'd better call your grandfather before we go any further with this."

He pushed the phone toward Tom who hesitated. It was all so unreal. Should he involve his grandfather, his family, in this? And how could he not? His hand was shaking as he dialed his grandfather's office.

When Tom had left Michael Shea's office, it was true

that no one had seen him. Michael Shea, wanting complete privacy during his showdown with Tom, had informed his nurse that he wouldn't be at the hospital until afternoon. She could have the half-day off. The main receptionist would keep a record of any calls for him. There had been no one in the immediate area of Shea's office. He had, in effect, signed his own death warrant.

Half an hour after Tom had left, another figure hurried silently down the hall to Shea's private office. The door opened. There sprawled on the floor lay Shea's body. As the figure bent over him, Shea stirred very slightly. A convulsive twitch contorted his body. He was not dead. His eyelids fluttered, but he did not open his eyes. He groaned. It was as though he were coming out of a long sleep. His disordered thoughts registered temporary defeat, but he had a sure sense that he would rise again. Michael Shea could not easily be kept down. Slowly he was regaining consciousness. Then there was a muffled shot, the report of a small-caliber pistol. The figure turned quickly and left the office. Michael Shea no longer moved.

It was one o'clock when Agnes Rhoades opened the door to Michael Shea's private office and saw his body on the floor. She screamed and fainted. Other people came running. A doctor was summoned. There was nothing to be done. This time Shea was dead. Agnes became hysterical. Someone called the police. The life and career of Dr. Michael Shea had come to an end.

On the flight to Mexico City, everything was going famously for Lisa. Jay Watson was a delightful traveling companion. They discovered they had so many things in common—books, theater, and the

Midwest. He had grown up in Illinois and attended the university there. She had probably witnessed football games at Champaign-Urbana when he was playing at left end. And he was wonderful with Chuckie. He played teddy bear games with him. He told stories.

"You must have children of your own," Lisa said. "You're so wonderful with Chuckie."

"My son and my wife were killed in an accident." His face was expressionless, but his eyes were haunted.

"I'm sorry."

"So am I," he said. "For a time I stopped living. But life goes on."

"And on and on and on," Lisa said.

He nodded. "And how long will you be in Mexico?" he asked.

"Indefinitely. I'm considering a Mexican divorce."

He ignored that. "And where will you be staying?"

She named her hotel.

"So touristy!"

"But I have friends in the city, Joan and Lester Coleman. They will show me the ropes."

He laughed. "I refuse to say 'small world,' but I know them. Lovely people. Check in, if you must, at that hotel, and then camp with them. We'll introduce you to the real Mexico City."

Lisa leaned back. Chuckie was asleep. The attentive man near her was ordering drinks for them from the hostess. What a cartwheel life was!

Chapter Eleven
Murder, Mexico, Marriages

Chris Hughes was not in the office when Tom's call from the police station came in. His secretary found Tom nearly incoherent, but she listened carefully, assured him that she would contact his grandfather as quickly as possible. She asked Tom to let her speak to the police sergeant. "Mr. Hughes isn't here right now. As soon as I reach him, he'll be on his way. Meanwhile I trust Tom will be made as comfortable as possible. He sounds so . . . well, disturbed."

"Don't worry, ma'am. We'll take care of him." The sergeant looked at Tom—the boy was shivering. "Sit down, son. All I need to know now is your name."

"Thomas Miller Hughes."

It was more than an hour before Chris Hughes's secretary succeeded in tracking him down. He was in a nearby town where a client had some property. As she repeated Tom's conversation to her, he listened intently. "Call the police station and tell them I'll be there as soon as possible. It should take me about thirty minutes," he directed.

By the time Chris Hughes got there, the police station was in a flurry of excitement. Michael Shea's body had been found and reported. The coroner was on his way to the death scene.

Chris Hughes put his arm around his grandson. "What happened, Tom?"

The boy shook his head. "It doesn't matter, Granddad. I killed him. I can't talk about it now."

The police sergeant approached them. "Sorry, Mr. Hughes. According to Dr. Shea's nurse, there had been trouble between the doctor and Tom. We'll have to book him on suspicion of murder."

Tom looked at him. "I killed Michael Shea."

"Try to get some rest, Tom," his grandfather said. "Relax if you can. I'll be here in the morning. You'll feel more like talking then. Meanwhile no more confessions, Tom. Oral or signed."

The boy winced at the words. His grandfather hugged him and left.

As Chris Hughes walked to his car, he shook his head in disbelief. Suddenly he felt old and tired and had a great need to talk this over with Nancy. He drove home. Nancy was at her desk writing a letter. He told her what little he knew. "I feel so helpless, so in the dark," he concluded.

For a time there was silence between them as Nancy fought for control. Concern for both Tom and her husband was uppermost. Memories of Tom raced through her mind. She and Chris had done their best to help Bob raise Tom. He'd been a rebellious child, but there had been reasons. They had wanted him to be happy and secure. They had tried to help him curb his temper. Had they failed so completely?

She looked at Chris. A younger Chris would have already been deciding on a course of action, formulating a strategy. She found it difficult to realize that her husband was almost seventy, that his energy level simply wasn't what it had been. Neither was hers, for that matter. But she was a practical woman. There was nothing to be gained by just sitting around and wringing one's hands. "Until Tom confides in us, there isn't much we can do. There'll be a coroner's report which we should see."

"Yes," Chris said. "Of course."

"And we should talk to the nurse who claims there was trouble between Tom and Michael Shea."

He nodded.

"And, Chris, I think you should assign this case to the brightest and best lawyer in the firm. That's you, of course," she added quickly, "but, my dear, I think you're too emotionally involved. Tom might even cooperate more with someone who isn't so personally involved."

"I'll call Roger Daniels," Chris said.

"There's no way of reaching Bob immediately. He's on a cross-country ski trip before starting his Vienna lectures. We should wait, anyway, until we know more."

Chris looked at her. "There's so much we don't know. Why did Tom kill him? Why?"

"That's what we must find out." She paused. "I wonder if the police have reached Lisa."

"I'll have Roger Daniels check on that."

Roger Daniels had been with the law firm of Lowell and Hughes for five years. He was bright, ambitious, and he had handled a number of cases brilliantly. Not yet forty, he was considered the heir apparent to Chris Hughes when he retired. He jumped at the chance to defend Tom Hughes.

Late in the afternoon, he had a long talk with Chris

and Nancy, learning all he could about their grandson. Then he went to the police station. The police had been unable to contact Mrs. Michael Shea. She and her son were in Mexico City. The Oakdale Travel Agency had booked her at the Hotel del Prado, but she had not checked in. The coroner's report was available. It stated that Michael Shea had died of head injuries.

There was an irony here that Roger Daniels had no way of detecting. The coroner, a Dr. Ragsdale, had received his appointment because of Michael Shea's influence. His incompetence staggered the imagination, but Michael had owed him a favor. When Dr. Ragsdale examined Michael's body, he was too befuddled by drink to notice the small, neat bullet hole just behind the ear. The head injuries were more noticeable and received whatever inspection he was able to give them. Shea was dead—of that there was no doubt. There was much blood from a nasty gash on the back of the head. *Voilà!* Cause of death—head injuries.

Lisa had not checked in at Hotel del Prado at the instigation of Jay Watson. He had talked her out of it as they flew towards Mexico City.

"To begin with," Jay Watson said, "Chuckie will hate being cooped up in a hotel room."

Lisa agreed.

"And I'll be miserable thinking of all the problems you'll have with a hotel existence in a city you're unacquainted with."

"Your concern is overwhelming, Mr. Watson."

"I'm serious," he said. "There's such a simple solution. Why not come to my hacienda? I have a guest cottage. I can even supply a servant who speaks some English." He smiled persuasively.

She hesitated.

"Be sensible, Lisa, and be my guest. No strings attached." He held up his right hand. "Scout's honor." He went on persuasively, "At least stay until you locate your friends."

Well, why not? she thought. She had to admit that the prospect of fending for herself and Chuckie in a strange place was a bit frightening. Here was a knight offering to rescue her. Instinctively she felt that she could trust him, and if there were entanglements . . . ? She looked at him—handsome, lithe, entertaining, ready to help. If an entanglement eventually came along, that might not be so bad either.

When they landed at International Airport, she collected her luggage and waited with Jay for the car he said would soon be there to pick them up. It was such a relief not to have to worry about even the small problems connected with arriving in a new country. As if by magic, he obtained a tourist card for her. He knew where to go and what to do. There was no confusion.

As they drove the few miles into the city, he pointed out places of interest. They reached the Zócalo, a great central square in the heart of the city. "This was the site of the Aztec capital," he said. "Over there is the National Cathedral, the oldest Christian church in North America."

"You sound like a tour guide," she told him, but she loved it. The buildings were breathtaking with their rich mosaics of Indian designs and symbols, and towering above them on the horizon were the snowy crests of Popocatepetl and Ixtacihuatl.

"I love Mexico," he said, with evident sincerity. "And there's so much I want to show you."

It was early evening when they reached Jay's place on the outskirts of the city. Lisa was impressed. The house itself, built in Spanish colonial style, was of stone with wrought-iron balconies opening onto a patio bright with flowers, gnarled vines, and a fountain. Servants carried her luggage and the small trunk on ahead to the guest house, while Jay showed her down the short winding path. Chuckie, clutching his teddy bear, was just ahead of them.

It was an adobe house with thick gray walls and a red-tiled roof. Large vine-like geraniums were afire with blooms on either side of the door. The central room was spacious. In a large fireplace, a fire was blazing.

"It gets quite cold at night," Jay said.

She surveyed the room with its dark, heavy furniture, the brightly colored glass shades on the lights, and the tiled floor with woven mats here and there. "Charming," she said. "You may have guests who refuse to leave."

He smiled. "We'll have a light supper in about an hour. I'll come for you. Meanwhile here's Juana to help you settle in." He introduced her to a dark-haired, smiling girl who suddenly appeared at his side.

When Jay arrived for them later, he carried a basket of toys. "Some things for Chuckie to enjoy. They belonged to my son."

She was touched. She turned her head from him quickly so he wouldn't see that her eyes had filled with tears.

Supper was light, simple, and good. "And now I know you must be tired," he said as they finished their coffee. Chuckie was already asleep on her lap. "Tomorrow we'll make plans for some sightseeing."

It was only as she was drifting off to sleep that she

remembered she'd forgotten to cancel her reservation at the hotel. Oh, well, she thought to herself, mañana.

At breakfast the next morning, Jay had a surprise. "I phoned the Colemans. They're delighted you're here, and we've planned a short trip. First we'll go to Cuernavaca to see the four hundred-year-old palace which Hernando Cortes built, and the double pyramid. Then on to Taxco, the silver city. Next day we'll drive to Puebla. It's called the city of ceramics. You'll love it. And as we start back, we'll stop by Cholula, which was the holy city of the Aztecs."

"Wonderful," Lisa said, "but what about my hotel reservations?"

"I took the liberty of canceling them."

So the pleasant three-or-four-day trip was arranged. They left the next morning, blithely unaware that the Oakdale police and Roger Daniels were desperately trying to locate Lisa.

Back in Oakdale there was a great amount of talk about Tom Hughes's forthcoming murder trial and the disappearance of Lisa Shea. Most people found it difficult to believe that Michael Shea could give anyone cause to murder him. Here and there a few people who had seen the side of Michael Shea that he had successfully hidden from the general public were not so surprised. But Tom Hughes a murderer? Incredible! True, the boy had been in a scrap or two, but he had never seemed the violent type. They shook their heads. The Vietnam experience did strange things to some of the young men who had served there.

Roger Daniels went about his job with painstaking care. He learned that Tom had been known to take drugs, but he couldn't uncover any criminal connections. Apparently the boy didn't owe large sums of money, and he hadn't reneged on any promises or arrangements.

Tom himself was completely uncooperative. He refused to say why he had attacked Michael Shea, except that it was something personal between them. He denied it had been a case of self-defense. "I killed him," he said repeatedly. "I'm willing to accept the consequences."

Obviously there must have been a link between the fact that Lisa Shea was Michael Shea's wife and Tom Hughes's mother. Roger Daniels found nothing but blind alleys when he tried to explore this situation. It was maddening that no one could find Lisa. The police in Mexico City were polite and claimed they were doing their best to discover her whereabouts, but Roger wondered how thorough a job they were doing.

He went to Chris Hughes. "Do you think we should send someone to Mexico City? Someone we could be sure would be doing his utmost to find Lisa Shea and Chuckie?"

Chris Hughes considered the question carefully. His opinion of Lisa Shea was not the highest. He had never forgiven her for trapping his son into marriage and then deserting him and their son for another man. He doubted that she could be helpful. "Let's wait a few days. I think we should concentrate on Tom's case. I'm positive that Tom did not go to Shea's office intending to kill him. The death was accidental. But what provoked Tom to attack him?" He shook his head. He was still too stunned to think clearly.

At home he talked to Nancy. What did she think? "I've done some sleuthing myself. I talked to Mrs. Fuller, Lisa's housekeeper. She doesn't know where Lisa and Chuckie are, but she gave me one bit of information that Roger Daniels should know. Lisa wasn't just taking a vacation—she was leaving Michael."

Chris smiled wearily. "Lisa has a habit of leaving people. But you're right, this is useful information. I think we should confront Tom with it. Did he know Lisa was leaving Michael Shea? Did he know why?" He sighed. "It's all so confusing, but I'll tell Roger about it."

She decided to change the subject. Poor Chris. He looked so tired. She would give him something lighter to think about. "This came in the mail today." She handed him an envelope. It was an invitation to the wedding of Liz and Dan Stewart. "Do you think we should go?"

"I think our presence might dampen the festive spirit. Why don't you send regrets?"

Spirits were festive indeed. Liz and Dan had decided on a small wedding, and Liz was busy redecorating the parlor where they would be married. She was not trying to erase the memory of Paul. She would never do that, but there had been much unhappiness here. She wanted to brighten things, to make it all look different. The painting was done and the new wall-to-wall carpeting was down. She was very pleased with the beige drapes and today the newly upholstered chairs and divan were due to arrive. It had been a busy time and Wade's Bookstore had suffered as a result, but she had great confidence in the two women who were running the place in her absence.

Liz could not have ordered a prettier wedding day. Fresh snow had fallen the night before and sparkled clean and white in the brilliant sunlight. It was cold, but not bitterly so. By three, everything was ready. The ladies in the kitchen moved the wedding cake to the dining room. The champagne was iced. In the living room daffodils added a burst of color.

Ellen and David Stewart were among the first of the guests. The others, all close friends, were there by four o'clock. Happiness permeated the room.

The champagne was served. The bride and groom cut the cake and were toasted by all, including Betsy with her Shirley Temple complete with maraschino cherry.

"I've never seen Dan happier," Ellen told David Stewart. "It does my heart good."

The doorbell rang in the midst of all the excitement. David Stewart answered it. The young man standing there was a reporter from the Oakdale paper. A photographer was with him. The wedding of one of Memorial Hospital's most popular doctors with the owner of Wade's Bookstore was news. He would like to talk with them briefly and take a few pictures. "Why don't you wait awhile until most of the guests have left?" David Stewart suggested. "Have some champagne and a piece of cake." They accepted.

In an hour or so all the guests except Ellen and David Stewart had left. The reporter approached Liz and Dan, introduced himself, and began with a few routine questions. Then perhaps because he had over-indulged in champagne, his questions became bolder.

"Mr. Stewart, do you plan to adopt little Betsy? Will your daughter, Emily, be staying on here?"

Dan stared at him coldly and didn't answer.

"If you'd like a couple of pictures now—" Liz began.

The reporter cut in, "Did you know that the former Mrs. Stewart—Susan, that is—just remarried? The paper's carrying an item on it in tomorrow's edition. We'll be sure to keep the pieces on separate pages. You'll rate page one."

Liz smiled. "We wish her every happiness. Let's take the pictures now."

The photographer snapped his pictures. They left.

Ellen, who had overheard the reporter, turned to Liz and Dan. "So Susan had someone waiting in the wings. I'm not too surprised."

"Congratulations, Dan," David Stewart said. "Your alimony payments stop before they begin."

Dan smiled wryly. "It really doesn't matter. The settlement included the house." His mind raced with questions that couldn't be answered. Would Susan and Mr. Whoever-He-Was live in Oakdale now? Would she change her mind about Emily? That would mean a legal fight. She had handed over the custody of the child to him in Chris Hughes's law office.

That whole situation had been so strange. Susan had lost one child and yet when Emily came along, she hadn't seemed involved with her at all. She had no great emotional attachment to her. The housekeeper-nanny seemed to love her more. Susan didn't even seem to care much about letting Dan have custody of Emily. Would she change now?

For the moment, Dan refused to worry. The important thing was that he and Liz were married. Nothing was going to mar their happiness.

They stood together in the doorway and waved goodbye to Ellen and David and to Betsy, who was spending the night with them.

"Do you know what I'd like now?" Liz asked.

"Yes, I do."

"What?"

"A pot of tea."

She smiled and kissed him. "You're absolutely correct," she said. "And then, my dear husband, I'll be ready for anything. Anything at all!"

Chapter Twelve
Love And Loss

The days raced by for Liz and Dan. As a wedding present, they had given each other an uninterrupted week. Wade's Bookstore would not see Liz. Memorial General would not see Dan. They would see only each other. Emily's nurse had agreed to look after Betsy, and the two little girls became better acquainted as they stayed in the house that was now Susan's. There had been no word from her. She and her new husband must be honeymooning too. Dan hoped they were in Timbuktu.

It was late March, and spring suddenly made its benign presence felt in Oakdale. The snow melted. Crocuses and anemones bloomed. "It's as though nature is giving us a special treat for a wedding present," Liz said.

Each day was a new adventure. Each night was blissfully exciting. They were happy in love. "I feel young and foolish," Dan told her. "I'd like to dress you in silks and satins and throw emeralds at your feet."

Liz made a face. "They'd crunch when I walked. I'd

much rather have a new spring outfit from Renée's."

They went on shopping expeditions and bought silly, impractical gifts—a medicine ball for Dan, a huge teapot for Liz and a case of tea.

The spring weather stayed. One morning, they spent three solid hours in the Oakdale seed store. They were busy buying seeds for the ambitious vegetable garden they planned for summer and the flower garden that would transplant a bit of England to Oakdale. Both of them enjoyed cooking. They worked together to create gourmet dinners for two by candlelight and they toasted each other and the wonderful future they would share together. It was a week of sheer magic, of joyful togetherness that exceeded all their expectations. They laughed, they loved, and they looked at each day as a special present just for them.

"It was the loveliest of honeymoons," Liz said on the last night of their "gift" week. Tomorrow Wade's Bookstore and Memorial General would become reality again.

They had decided to install Mrs. Shore, Emily's nurse, in their home. "A live-in nanny," Liz said. Mrs. Shore was delighted. She and Emily and Betsy would move in tomorrow. "The little girls get along beautifully," Mrs. Shore reported. "They both are treasures."

Both the bookstore and the hospital had problems waiting for Liz and Dan when they returned to work. "We didn't want to worry you on your honeymoon," the temporary managers told Liz, "but there's a rumor that Oakdale will soon have another bookstore."

"Maybe the competition will be good for us," Liz responded. "And I think most of our customers will be loyal."

Both women shook their heads. "It isn't so much the idea of competition," one of them said.

"The problem is the competitor," the other one finished.

Liz waited.

"They say," the first went on, "that a Mr. Bell will be the owner. He's had a very successful store in Chicago and will be moving here."

"And who is Mr. Bell?" Liz asked.

"Mr. Bell," the woman said, "is the new husband of the former Mrs. Stewart."

Liz tried to cloak her surprise. So Susan would be moving back to Oakdale, after all. Did this mean she would try to regain custody of Emily?

The ladies had more. "Mr. Bell has leased a building from Mr. Hart in the new shopping mall," the first one said. "And Mr. Hart has told several people that Mr. Bell predicted he would run Wade's Bookstore out of business."

Liz smiled a bit grimly. "We'll see about that. Meanwhile it's back to work and business as usual." Already she was considering new ways to lure customers to Wade's—a special book club for Wade's customers, a service to find out-of-print and rare books. And she would check immediately on the Bell bookstore in Chicago.

At Memorial General, in addition to his backlog of patients, Dan discovered that he had been elected by the board to find a replacement for Michael Shea. This would mean many telephone calls and interviews. In all likelihood, there would be a number of trips out of town, just at a time when he wanted most to be at home. He frowned. If Bob Hughes were only at hand, it would be so much easier.

No one had been able to track down Lisa Shea, but the hospital had contacted Michael Shea's mother in Memphis. She was due today, and Dan had been tapped to talk with her and to accompany her to the memorial service arranged for the afternoon. Mrs. Shea was brought to Dan's office just before noon. A rather pretty, wispy woman, small-boned, her blue eyes filled with tears when she was introduced to Dan.

She held his hand. "So you worked with mah Michael?" He nodded. "Why would anyone want to kill such a deah, sweet boy?" She started sobbing. He seated her in a chair and tried to comfort her as best he could. He praised Michael as a doctor and told her how proud she must be of him.

"Oh, Ah am. Ah am." She wiped her eyes with a dainty lace handkerchief. "Ah understand they haven't been able to contact his wife yet and deah little Chuckie?"

"Not yet."

She launched into reminiscences of Michael as a little boy, of his determination to make something of himself, of his scholarships. "And now it's come to this." She wept again.

He suggested lunch. Gratefully she accepted and ate amazingly well for one so grief-stricken. The memorial service was blessedly brief. It was well-attended, but Dan had the feeling that curiosity had brought more people there than friendship for the late Dr. Michael Shea. Michael's mother seemed more composed than she had been earlier. She was riding back with the friends from Chicago who had brought her here. Her plans were to visit with them until Lisa Shea and Chuckie returned, whenever that might be. And when might that be?

* * *

Lisa was having a marvelous time in Mexico. She had forgotten how much fun the Colemans were. Joan and Lester were spur-of-the-moment people, and so was Jay Watson. Open-air markets were stop signs to them; they couldn't bear to pass them by. The station wagon bulged alarmingly with baskets and bowls. After Taxco they were all weighted down with silver. Joan Coleman was wonderful with Chuckie, a built-in babysitter.

It was the fourth night out when they stopped in Tlaxcala. The town was aglitter with a festival of some sort and although it was crowded, the Colemans found a small, picturesque inn with rooms for all. They walked up and down the bunting-draped streets, stopped to watch jugglers and acrobats and mimes, and listened to strolling musicians.

"I'm tired," Joan Coleman said. "Lester and I will go back to the inn and take Chuckie with us. You and Jay enjoy the fun. The night's young."

It was a beautiful, star-bright night. Lisa and Jay strolled up and down a few more streets and then stopped for tequila in a small nightclub boasting a string band that played with more charm than melody. They danced. When they returned to the table, Jay took her hand in his. "I'm falling in love with you, Lisa Shea," he said quietly.

She gazed into his eyes. "You promised there'd be no strings attached," she reminded him. "Scout's honor," she quoted.

He smiled. "No strings," he repeated. "But give me a chance, Lisa. When we return tomorrow, stay a while longer please."

"Jay, Jay!" She did not remove her hand from his. "There's so much you don't know about me. I've had what you might call a checkered past."

He put his hand to her lips. "We all have our guilts, if we've lived at all. Made our mistakes. Resolved to do better. And," he continued, "I think we do become 'better,' whatever that may mean."

"You're a very open person, Jay Watson. Very forthright. Very handsome. You turn a girl's head." She corrected herself. "A woman's head. In addition to Chuckie, I have a grown son."

He withdrew his hand from hers. "Truth time." He stated it, rather than asked, and held forth his tequila glass to her. "Have you noticed, I only nurse a drink, while others enjoy? I left out one fact about my wife and son's death. When they were killed in the accident, I was driving. Drunk."

What could she say? She looked at this intense, sensitive, handsome man. Once again her eyes glistened with tears, but this time, she did not turn away. "I think I may be falling in love with you, too, Jay. But I don't trust my heart anymore. It's led me astray so many times."

"Don't trust your heart," he said. "Trust me."

She shook her head. "It's all too sudden. We aren't kids, Jay."

He reached for her hand again. "That's the point, Lisa. Come back to my place. Stay awhile. We'll stop playing the tourist game and really get acquainted. We'll share secrets or not share them. I don't care about your past, Lisa. I want to be involved in your future, our future."

Crazy, she thought as she looked at him. *He's made me feel like a young girl again, being wooed for the first time*. It was quite incredible and yet at that moment, she had never felt so in control, so sure of herself. A new Lisa, with a new chance for happiness, was emerging. All the past, the old mistakes, could be forgotten, perhaps even forgiven eventually.

Jay said, "You've been miles away in your thoughts. Tell me about your older son. The one you say is grown up."

She thought of Tom. Sweet, rebellious Tom with his talent for causing trouble for everyone. He'd never been an endearing little boy. Mad at the world, she thought. But it was not a world that he had created.

"Tom," she said to Jay, "is my child, but it took a long time for me to love him. I don't love easily," she added, "but when I do, watch out."

Jay smiled. "This is getting acquainted," he responded.

"I still don't know Tom," Lisa said, and then in a moment of honesty she added, "I deserted him when I shouldn't have, but he's a good boy, I think. Reaching out for love." The words embarrassed her. She sipped her drink and smiled. "Let's talk about us."

Tom Hughes sat in his cell and thought, *I've never been so alone in my life.* But he also kept saying, *I mustn't feel sorry for myself.* Yet he did. Alone in a prison cell. He had built the cell around himself, or had he? There had been no intent on his part to kill Michael Shea as they drove to Memorial Hospital. But the man had turned out to be so evil! He'd needed to be hammered down, but not killed.

Perhaps, he thought, he was wrong in not telling his grandfather and Roger Daniels, who were trying so hard to help him, about the secret Shea had held over his head. How he wished for his mother! Proud, arrogant, vibrant Lisa, who could slam doors and unlock doors, who could run away and come back. Where was she now? Hadn't she heard about his predicament? He swatted at a cockroach that ran up the cell wall and missed. He always missed.

There was no point in brooding. When his mother had called him, she had told him to look after his grandmother. And the jailer had given him writing material in case he wanted to write a letter. Did Alma Miller know what had happened to him? He wondered. Should he tell her? Picking up paper and pen, he wrote to her.

> You probably have heard of the trouble I'm in. Believe me, I didn't plan to kill Michael Shea, but it happened, and I'm responsible. Please don't worry about me. Grandfather Hughes has assigned a very good lawyer, Roger Daniels, to my case. Do you know where my mother is? I wish she were here . . .

He gave the letter to the guard on duty who promised to mail it immediately.

Annie received Tom's letter the next day. She stared at the envelope and debated as to whether or not she should give it to Alma Miller. She had told Alma about Tom, minimizing the situation as much as she could. Michael Shea had died accidentally, and Tom was involved in the accident. The police were holding Tom until they learned more.

Mrs. Miller hadn't seemed to understand. Since Annie had come to stay with her, she had gradually declined. Most of the time she lay in bed with her eyes closed. Annie couldn't tell if she was asleep or just shutting out the world.

When Mr. Daniels had been there the day before, he had found it difficult to get much information. Annie had given him the Mexico City number that Lisa had also given them to call in case of emergency.

Roger Daniels had studied it. "Hotel del Prado," he said. "The travel agency gave us that number too.

We've called repeatedly. She never checked in."

Now Annie told Alma about receiving Tom's letter, and Alma ordered her to read it to her.

"You try that Mexico City number again," she ordered Annie.

Annie tried and this time, she got through. The voice from the Del Prado came through clearly. Lisa's reservation there had been cancelled by a friend. Annie got the name of the friend, a man named Jay Watson, but they had no address for him.

When Annie hung up, Alma's eyes were wide open. She even had some color in her cheeks.

Alma told Annie, "Call what's-his name. That man who was here. Tell him we have a letter from Tom he should see and a little information about Lisa. Tell him to high-tail it out here." She sank back on her pillows, exhausted.

"I'll be right out," Roger Daniels said when Annie called him, regretting not at all giving up a free Saturday afternoon. Maybe, just maybe, this case is opening up a bit, he thought. Somehow he felt if they could find Lisa, things would start falling into place. There was so little time, really. The Oakdale district attorney, eager for the publicity while the case was still fresh in the public's mind, had succeeded in getting the trial scheduled on the court calendar in two more weeks. Roger Daniels's appeal for delay had failed. He prayed that "the little information" Alma and Annie had about Lisa would lead to the discovery of her whereabouts.

The fascinating trip with the Colemans and Jay Watson had ended for Lisa. The Colemans returned to their home after making Lisa promise that she'd visit them the following week. They would take her to see the floating gardens of Xochimilco. They were a must, they told her.

And here she was back in the guest house. There were things at the office that needed Jay's attention, so he was usually gone by the time she and Chuckie went to the main house for breakfast. She missed him during the day, but there was so much to fill her time. He had provided a pony for Chuckie, and a horse for her. She kept promising herself that she would write to Tom and to her mother.

Jay was usually back home by early evening. Over drinks one evening, she told him, "I haven't been so relaxed and so refreshed in years."

"It's the Mexican tempo," he said.

They took long walks. They held long talks. He told her of his boyhood. When they said good night at the guest house door, he held her close and kissed her, but he was patient. He had promised "no strings attached," and he would keep his promise until she released him from it.

Lisa found it difficult to remember that she was still married to Michael Shea. I must start investigating a Mexican divorce, she told herself, and then sighed dreamily. Mañana. It was the Mexican tempo.

The tempo in Oakdale was not so relaxed. Liz had checked out the Bell bookstore in Chicago. It was true that it was quite successful and also true that Mr. Bell was moving the stock to Oakdale. His lease was up in Chicago. He had found an ideal spot in Oakdale, according to the manager with whom Liz had talked.

Then quite unexpectedly one Saturday morning, Dan telephoned from the hospital. He'd had a call from Susan. She would be in Oakdale that afternoon and suggested that they meet in Liz's office at the bookstore. No, she didn't want to see him at Memorial General. The bookstore would be more convenient for her, she'd insisted.

Susan arrived promptly at three. In tow was Mr. Bell. Introductions were made all around. Vincent Bell was older than Liz and Dan had expected. He was well into his fifties, they would guess, and a little rough around the edges. His sports coat and his voice were both too loud. He was overweight and overbearing. "Well, little lady," he addressed Liz, "I'm gonna give you a real run for yer money. Yer lah-de-dah bookstore is gonna find it's not easy competing with a big-city enterprise that knows what the public wants."

Liz smiled. "We'll do our best to make it interesting for you, Mr. Bell."

Susan cut in. "That's not the main issue now, Vincent," she said with a pained expression. She turned to Dan. "When can we move into the house?"

"I assume it's ready unless you intend to do some redecorating," he answered. "Everything that's mine has been removed. You can check the list with someone at Chris Hughes's firm. I doubt if Chris is available right now."

Susan shuddered. "I heard about it. Dreadful. Michael was such a dear boy."

"Will you be returning to Memorial?" Dan asked her.

"I haven't decided yet," Susan replied.

It struck Liz as bizarre that Susan had made not one inquiry about the daughter she had not seen for weeks. "Aren't you going to ask about Emily?"

"How's Emily?" Susan snapped.

"Lovely," Liz answered smoothly. "Growing like a weed. She and Betsy get along famously, and Mrs. Shore is a gem."

"Of course," remarked Susan. "I knew when I hired her that she was one in a million."

"Wouldn't you like to see Emily?" Dan put in.

Susan hesitated. She and Vincent Bell exchanged glances. Evidently the subject of Emily had been discussed previously. "I don't think so," she said. "Seeing me would only confuse her. When she's older, perhaps we can get acquainted, but for now . . ." She looked at Vincent again and didn't complete the sentence.

"I understand," Dan said, not unkindly. It seemed obvious that Vincent Bell had put his foot down about visits to or from Emily.

"Would you care for some tea?" Liz asked in the politest of voices.

Vincent Bell laughed. "Tea now," he said. "If you don't mind, ducky, I think we'll make a break for it and find us a drink. See you in the funny papers!"

The goodbyes were hurried.

"Thank God it's Saturday," Liz remarked. "We're going to need Sunday to recover from this."

Dan shook his head. "I can't believe Vincent Bell. Do you think you'll be competing with a porno bookstore?"

Liz laughed. "Are you going back to Memorial?"

"No," Dan told her. "If there's such a thing as a good book around this place, I'll curl up with it until closing time. And then, Mrs. Stewart, I'll take you to the nearest pub for drinks and dinner. It's the least I can do after putting you through this encounter with Susan and Vincent."

They were home by ten o'clock. Both of them looked in on the little girls sound asleep, smiling faintly. "I think they're dreaming of sugar plums," Liz whispered.

"More likely they're dreaming of tomorrow's expedition. Mrs. Shore has promised to take them to her brother's place in the country. They love it there."

It had been a tiring day. They turned in early. At three o'clock, Dan was awakened by the sound of Liz trying unsuccessfully to smother her giggles.

"What is it?" he asked sleepily.

"Oh, Dan, I'm sorry, but I dreamed about Vincent Bell. We were in the funny papers together and he kept calling me 'ducky.' It woke me up."

He was fully awake now too. "I won't have another man in your life," he said huskily. He took her in his arms. She was so warm and vibrant and full of life. He pressed against her, feeling the excitement of his body and the response of hers. They caressed each other and kissed. Their lovemaking had never been so passionate, so complete, so satisfying. They held each other close long after the tidal wave of passion had ebbed. Words were not needed. The vocabulary of love had exceeded anything they might say.

Liz was the first to wake up the next morning. She lay in bed and listened to the excited babble as the little girls left, and Mrs. Shore tried to hush them. The car drove away and still Dan slept. He was a handsome man and asleep he looked so vulnerable, so little-boyish, even with the dark stubble of early-morning whiskers. Quietly she eased out of bed. In the shower she thought of last night and their lovemaking. She hoped for another baby soon — a little boy, just like Dan. Slipping into her most special dressing gown, she tiptoed through the bedroom. He was still asleep. Very well. She would surprise him with breakfast in bed.

When she came back upstairs, he was awake, surprised at the tray. As they ate breakfast, occasionally his foot found hers and gently nudged it.

"Delicious," he said. "Delicious, ducky."

"It's a beautiful day," she said. "What shall we do?"

"Stay in bed." He gave her a lascivious look.

"A lovely idea," she responded. "But first let me clear the scene for action." She slipped into her satin mules. The tray minus food was not so heavy now. She stacked dishes and balanced the load with care.

The crash came when she was just starting down the stairs. He bounded out of bed and found her in a crumpled heap halfway down. She stared at him, eyes wide with wonder. A stain of red widened beneath her. He could see the jagged edge of the broken teapot protruding from her side. "You're all right," he murmured. "Don't worry." Her eyes drooped shut and she fainted.

At the hospital they told him what he already knew. There was no change. Her liver was massively ruptured. There was no chance to save her. It was only a matter of hours. He stayed at her side until she died, and he died with her.

Someone had called Ellen and David Stewart. They were waiting in the hall when he came from her room. They led him outside to their car. It seemed impossible that it could still be a beautiful day.

There would be no funeral. They had never discussed it, but he knew instinctively that she would prefer cremation. Later, perhaps, there would be a memorial service. For the time being, he would stay on in their home. Mrs. Shore would continue to take care of Betsy and Emily. He would find a housekeeper.

Somehow he propelled himself through the days. At night he took long walks. Real spring had come. He tried to plant the garden they had planned, to create the English flower garden that Liz had envisioned. It was impossible for him. He hired a gardener.

Friends were wonderful. The staff at the bookstore assured him that they could run things until he decided what to do with the store. There were invitations galore. He worked long hours at the hospital. Still there was so much time now stretching on ahead endlessly. Condolences poured in—telegrams, cards, letters. He read them and appreciated them, but the words were meaningless. Eventually a small note-sized envelope came. The return address was one of those stickers that charity organizations mail out for contributions. It read "Mrs. Vincent Bell." The address was familiar, his old home. So Susan and Vincent had moved in. He held the envelope in his hand, but he did not open it. Later perhaps, but not now.

He smiled. Liz would have appreciated the irony of this. Ah, ducky! It was as though they could still share jokes.

Chapter Thirteen

Bad News

That Saturday—the day before Liz Stewart's death, though he could not know that—Roger Daniels had "high-tailed" it to Alma Miller's in less than an hour.

"She's asleep," Annie told him. "Not at all well, sir. Just sorta slips in and out."

"Horse apples," Alma called from the bedroom. "I'm wide awake. Come in, Mr. Whositz."

"Roger Daniels." He reintroduced himself.

She pulled Tom's letter from under her pillow. "What do you make of this? Will it be helpful?" She handed it to him.

Before he read it, he studied this gaunt woman before him. A glance confirmed that she was seriously ill, yet she had a surprising strength. She was fighting—fighting for her grandson. She was doomed, but Tom must have a chance. She was a perceptive woman. He read the letter. "This should be helpful. I think we have a strong case of death by accident."

"Lisa," Alma Miller said. "You must find Lisa."

"Did you ever hear her speak of Jay Watson?"

She withered him with a look of contempt. "If you've been on this case as long as you claim, you should know my Lisa by now. Jay Watson is probably some charmer she met on the flight to Mexico City, and Lisa is a pushover for charmers." She leaned back on her pillows and fought for breath. In a moment she shook a bony finger at him. "Michael Shea was a charmer." She indicted him without compassion. "One of the worst. I remember their wedding." She seemed to drift in and out of memories. "There was something very wrong that day. No one was happy. I baked a jim-dandy cake, and it was hardly touched. Something was wrong that day."

She had closed her eyes. Suddenly they opened again. "You still here?" she asked.

He nodded.

"Get goin' and find Jay Watson. Shouldn't be too hard. He'll be handsome, well-heeled, and well-known. Lisa never wasted her time with pikers."

Annie showed him out. "The doctor was here this morning," she said. "He told me Alma's failing fast. If you find Lisa, tell her about her mother."

He promised he would.

Finding the whereabouts of Jay Watson was not as difficult as Roger Daniels had expected. The man was well known in the business and social circles of Mexico City. It took just a couple of days for him to get Jay Watson's office number and his home phone number as well.

When he called, he was told, "Mr. Watson is on a short trip. He should be back in a day or so."

"Have him call me immediately," he directed.

Early the next morning, he visited Tom in the Oakdale jail. "Look, Tom, I've learned a number of things. Your mother was not on a spur-of-the-moment vacation. She was leaving Michael Shea."

Tom merely said, "I know."

"And she's with friends in the Mexico City area. Plans have changed. We're about to track her down."

Tom smiled. "I know Mom and her changing plans. So what else is new?"

Roger Daniels paused. "Your grandmother let me read your letter to her, Tom. We have it in your writing now that Michael Shea's murder was not premeditated."

Tom smiled more grimly and repeated, "So what else is new?"

Lisa was not the only one proving elusive. Nancy and Chris Hughes were completely frustrated in trying to track Bob down. They left messages scattered across Switzerland and Austria—at ski lodges, inns and hotels—to no avail. They knew, of course, that he was on a cross-country ski trip. Presumably the entire party was beleaguered in some remote place by a blizzard. But where? It was maddening.

Strangely enough Bob Hughes's European venture was similar to Lisa's Mexican experience. The ski party was not large, ten in all, including the guides. Most of them were doctors who had been attending the conference. Among them was Dr. Louise Bronson from London. She was tall, redheaded, with green eyes that shone with intelligence. Bob had immediately been drawn to her. An excellent skier, she usually was the first of the group behind the lead guide. Bob found it difficult to keep up with her, and it was impossible to converse as they trekked cross country.

But the nights were different. The first night out, they stopped at a lodge tucked away in a small valley high in the Alps. Before supper the group gathered in front of a huge fireplace for drinks. Bob maneuvered deftly and seemingly by chance next to Louise.

"Does anyone know how far we traveled today?" he asked her.

"We got off to a late start, but the guide said that we covered nearly fifty miles," she answered.

"I'm still out of breath," Bob said. "You're an excellent skier."

"At least for one who grew up in the flattest part of England."

"I grew up in very flat Illinois."

She smiled. "Actually my father came from Sweden, and he was a real ski enthusiast. We spent part of the season in Sweden every year."

They sat next to each other at the supper table and became better acquainted. She was an obstetrician and had a nice practice located on Charing Cross Road. He described his life at Memorial General. When they said good night, Bob bowed low and said, "You're the prettiest obstetrician I ever met."

She dimpled. "I have no way of knowing whether or not that's a compliment."

"It is," he assured her.

On the second night, they discovered that they both liked Mozart and enjoyed detective novels. He confessed that he didn't think much of Gilbert and Sullivan and she complained that she found Rodgers and Hammerstein too saccharine. More important, he learned that her first marriage had ended in divorce and that she had not remarried.

"My score is worse." He held up two fingers.

"You Americans," she said in mock disapproval.

The third day dawned bright and clear. There was no hint that the afternoon would usher in a fierce blizzard, unusually late in the year. They carried pack lunches and ate their noon meal in a tiny Alpine village where an occasional stray goat clattered by on the cobblestones and an old man pulling a milk cart stopped to sell his wares. "I keep expecting Heidi to come skipping down the street," Louise said.

A gray line of clouds advanced suddenly, obscuring the sun. The wind rose. They were at least two hours away from the village where they had lunched. The guides halted the party and consulted their maps. "Storm coming up fast," the lead guide told them. "There's a hamlet about an hour ahead. We'll try for that."

In another fifteen minutes the snow swirled in. For a while they skied on, but it was hard going. The fresh, soft snow bunched up against their skis. It stung their faces and clung to their goggles. Finally, the guides stopped and told them to unbuckle their skis. It would take longer, but going on foot would not be so exhausting. They fought their way, step by step, across the trackless snow. It was nightmarish. Each one held to the person just ahead. It was as though they walked in a white, whirling cloud. How did the guide know where he was leading them? Bob wondered. There were no landmarks, only the blowing, drifting snow. He felt as though they were walking in circles.

The lead guide turned to Louise, who was close behind him. "Buildings straight ahead," he yelled. "Pass the word along."

Slowly the buildings took form for them, like dark shadows through the snow. It was a cluster of houses, some sheds, and a barn. A few snow-laden, scraggly pines partially protected them. The lead guide banged on the door of the largest house, the rest of them bunched behind him, like a flock of sheep who had strayed too far from their fold.

It seemed an eternity before the door was opened. The guide quickly motioned them inside.

They were in luck. The chalet was at least large enough for them all to be tucked away for the duration of the storm. The guides assured the farmer and his wife that they would be well paid. There were provisions enough. No one would go hungry.

And oh, the wonderful warmth of it, the sanctuary of being inside, protected from the fury of the storm! "It's the most beautiful place I ever hope to see," Louise said.

Bob hugged her. Being with her was beautiful too.

For three days the storm raged. There were practical things to be done, and they all pitched in and helped. Armed with shovels, they worked with the farmer as he tunneled his way to the barn. They fed and watered the cows, and helped the farmer with all his chores.

That night the farmer discovered that one of the cows was in labor. It was not an easy birth. At first they took turns staying with the farmer and doing what they could. Three hours later when the calf was born, they were all there. Louise took charge, and she was triumphant. "I've just delivered my first calf, and he's a fine baby boy!" she exclaimed. "I've named him, too." She looked at Bob. "I'm calling him Bob Junior."

When they woke up in the morning, the snow had stopped. The world outside glistened in the bright sunshine. The lead guide went outside and came back to report. "Too powdery yet for skiing. It should thaw slightly today and then freeze over with a good crust. We'll stay here one more day, and then start out early in the morning."

Before they left the next day, Louise and Bob hurried out to say goodbye to Bob Jr. He was standing next to his mother. "Handsome devil, isn't he?" Bob stated, admiring his bovine namesake.

"Like you," Louise said.

The snow was perfect. They stayed side by side as they made their way through the snow. The scenery was breathtaking. Now and again they stopped to look and wonder. There was no need for words between them. Something else was leaving them breathless. They were in love.

The Oakdale courthouse was a hideous building of yellow brick. Square and solid, it stood facing a used-car lot and a pizza palace. Here on a Monday morning, a group of forty people had been summoned to select a jury to try the case of the State of Illinois versus Thomas Miller Hughes. It was a day of rain and wind, and the prospective jurors arrived wet and curious. Roger Daniels had tried to have the trial moved to another jurisdiction because of the publicity surrounding Michael Shea's death. He had been unsuccessful.

The tedious process of selecting jurors began. Tom Hughes watched stoically as the lawyers questioned this one and that one.

Two hours, and two jurors had been selected. This could go on for days. The judge recessed them for lunch.

Lisa greeted each new day eagerly. The thought occurred to her that she might like to live here permanently, and Jay Watson was certainly part of the picture. *Tomorrow definitely I'll start checking out how to proceed with a divorce*, she told herself. But today was too beautiful to waste on such a perplexing problem. "Hurry up, Chuckie," she said. "Let's go for a ride."

Her eyes reflected her enthusiasm.

Chuckie was on his pony and Lisa was on her horse as they rode along. "We're exploring," she told the little boy. "Maybe we'll find gold or dragons."

They found a dragon in the form of a rattlesnake coiled in the path in front of Chuckie's pony. The little horse reared, Chuckie toppled off, and the snake slithered away. Lisa was off her horse in a second and by Chuckie's side. He was crying. One look and she knew that his leg was broken.

She gave her horse a slap and he started back towards the house. The pony followed. She soothed Chuckie as best she could. She had to be calm. Looking about her, she found a stick that would serve her purpose. With her scarf and a belt, she strapped the broken leg clumsily but firmly to the stick. Fortunately, they hadn't gone far. Even more fortunately when the rideless horses had returned to the house, the servants started looking for them. They met her on the small path as she carried Chuckie home. A call to Jay helped matters even more. He directed her to the nearest doctor and said he'd meet them there.

It was not a bad fracture. By the time Jay got there, it was set and Chuckie's leg was in a cast. They carried Chuckie to the station wagon. He was sleepy from a sedative and feeling no pain. They would hire a nurse, Jay told her. He knew one who spoke English and he was sure Chuckie would like her. At home, the Colemans were waiting for them. Jay had phoned them about Chuckie and they had come to see if they could help.

The phone rang. It was a Roger Daniels calling from Oakdale, Illinois. Obviously, the messages he had asked to be delivered to Jay Watson had gone astray.

He was making another effort to contact him and this time, much to his relief, he succeeded.

Jay listened intently. Then he said, "Lisa is here. I think you should talk directly to her. Just wait a minute." He motioned to Lisa and to the Colemans. "There's bad news from Oakdale, Lisa. Brace yourself."

Roger Daniels was as considerate as he could be. He didn't shock Lisa with everything at once. First he told her, "There's been an unfortunate accident here. I regret that I'm the one to tell you. Michael Shea is dead."

Lisa's voice was steady. "I see." She didn't see at all, of course, but one had to say something. "When did this happen?"

"A couple of weeks ago, Mrs. Shea. We've been trying to reach you ever since you arrived in Mexico City."

She tried to think clearly. "Then there's been a funeral service, a burial, all the arrangements?"

"There was a memorial service, Mrs. Shea. But you're needed back here now."

Lisa considered. "Mr. Daniels, I realize that I must come back, that there are things to be settled. But surely there's no immediate urgency. My little boy broke his leg just this afternoon. I'd like to stay with him a few days at the very least."

A pause, and then Roger Daniels said, "Mrs. Shea, you're needed back here now, believe me."

Lisa caught the urgency in his voice and asked him who he was. When he told her that he was with Chris Hughes's law firm, she began to feel cold and frightened. She knew something was wrong and as she pressed him, he told her the whole story slowly.

She hung up and faced Jay and the Colemans. "My son Tom is accused of murdering my husband."

Jay held her in his arms as she struggled to keep herself in control. Carefully she repeated her conversation with Roger Daniels, as if to reinforce her memory. "Michael Shea was an evil person," she told them. "Tom was his victim . . . so was I . . . and I'm sure there were others. Now I must get there."

The Colemans assured her that they would be on hand to watch over Chuckie. "We'll be leaving here in another month. We can bring him with us then. Don't worry." Jay was already at work on reservations to Chicago. Juana was packing her bags.

"You're all being magnificent," she told them. Chuckie was asleep. The nurse had arrived almost magically.

On the way to the airport, she leaned against Jay. A great fatigue had overtaken her, but she didn't sleep. "I'll call you when I get to Chicago," she told him. "Jay, I've asked so much of you, but there's one thing more."

"Anything."

"Could you get the name of the best detective agency in Chicago? I plan an investigation of my own. I simply can't believe that Tom could have killed Michael in a silly fight."

"I'll have the information by the time you call."

He stayed with her until it was time to board the plane. "Call me every day," he told her. "You give me a report on you and I'll give a report on Chuckie."

She promised and kissed him goodbye.

He watched her as she walked away. A magnificent woman, he thought, strong and honest, and how wonderful that she had turned to him for help. He strained for a last glimpse of her. She turned and waved. A somber thought occurred to him that she might well be walking out of his life, but he discarded such thinking immediately. This thing that was happening was temporary. She would be back. They would share a wonderful life together.

After Roger Daniels spoke with Lisa, he called Annie. "Tell her mother that we've found Lisa. She's on her way to Oakdale."

"Thank God," Annie said.

"How is Mrs. Miller?"

Annie lowered her voice. "She's a very sick woman, Mr. Daniels. Did you tell Lisa about her mother?"

He explained why he hadn't. "But when I meet her, I will," he promised. From a distance he could hear Alma Miller's voice. "Tell Mr. Daniels that he and Lisa must concentrate on Tom."

He smiled. "Tell Mrs. Miller that we will."

Marvel Shea, Michael's mother, had made him promise that he would let her know if Lisa had been contacted. He called her. She was relieved to know that Lisa had been found, but disappointed that Chuckie would not be with her. Eager to see Lisa, she suggested that she accompany Mr. Daniels to the airport or meet him there. "It will be very late, Mrs. Shea."

"Ah'm quite a night owl. Really, Ah am."

After the call, she turned to her friends. "Ah have the feelin' that they don't want me around. Ah imagine they think that Michael's sweet little mother in the courtroom might create considerable sympathy, and that's exactly what Ah intend to do."

When Lisa arrived in Chicago, Roger Daniels was waiting. "I want to call friends in Mexico City to tell them I'm here safe and sound."

Jay answered the phone immediately. Assured that all was well with her and assuring her that Chuckie was doing fine, he gave her the name of the Chicago detective agency that he'd found. "They'll be expecting a call from you in the morning. I gave them a brief outline of the problem."

"I couldn't cope with this without you, Jay."

"At your service, ma'am."

"Jay, do you realize that I'm a widow now?"

"Not for long, my dear, if I have anything to do with it."

They said good night.

She returned to Roger Daniels. "This is awkward," she told him. "I don't know how to say it."

"Just say it."

"I think you've been doing a great job, but I'm launching an investigation of my own. In the morning I have an appointment at a detective agency."

"What agency and what time?"

"Delacourt at ten o'clock."

"I know them. They're good. And there's no problem. I'll drive you to your mother's tonight, and then in the morning we'll come back to Chicago."

On the trip to Alma Miller's, he told Lisa that her mother's condition had worsened. "Be prepared for a bit of a shock," he said.

The sight of her mother, so wasted and pale, was something that Lisa had not bargained for. Alma Miller held her hand and patted it. "Don't worry, baby. Things are going to turn out right."

Lisa fought back the tears.

Alma smiled. "Old, sick people have a way of knowing things. There's time to think things through as you lie here. Tom's a good boy. Did you know he wrote me a letter?"

Lisa nodded.

Her mother closed her eyes and Lisa thought she might have gone to sleep, but she spoke again. "I had a dream, Lisa. Tom didn't kill Michael Shea." She paused. When she spoke again, her voice, which had been so weak, was firm and resolute. "Michael Shea killed Michael Shea." This time she did not reopen her eyes. Lisa sat by the bed several minutes, gazing at this frail woman who was so dear to her. Her mother was sleeping, breathing more easily. Tenderly she kissed her on the cheek and tiptoed out of the room.

She was bone-weary. Roger Daniels had already gone to sleep on the couch in what Alma called her flower room. Annie hovered nearby. "I've turned down the bed for you, Lisa."

"Annie, Annie, thank you for all you've done." She kissed her and said good night.

In the morning Annie had a farmhand's breakfast ready for them. "Your mom is still asleep," she informed Lisa. "Best night's rest she's had in weeks."

When they left, Alma Miller was still asleep. "Tell her goodbye for me." Lisa said. "I'll be back as soon as possible."

At the detective agency she found that they had already assigned two men to the case, pending her approval.

She met them, Lee Banks and Dave Kent. They were black and young and very serious. She told them all she knew and they listened carefully, taking notes, asking penetrating questions. She liked them.

Banks and Kent promised to report the next morning in Oakdale. She gave them the address of her home and realized suddenly it would be her first time back there since she had left with Chuckie for Mexico City. So much had happened.

Returning to the house was not as traumatic as she had expected. Roger Daniels helped her in with her luggage. He would be back in the morning to share what he knew with the detectives.

She turned on all the lights. Someone had cleaned the house. It was spotless. Fresh linen was on her bed. Towels hung neatly in the bathroom. She found a can of soup in the cupboard and fixed herself a bowl. She had just finished it when the doorbell rang.

She opened the door. Two little girls stood there, each with a basket of flowers. She was perplexed until she remembered. It was May Day, of course. "How lovely," she said. "Won't you come in while I see if I can't find some candy?" A figure stepped out of the shadows. "That won't be necessary, Lisa."

"Dan! Dan Stewart! And these are your daughters."

He introduced her to Emily and Betsy, as she invited them in.

"I'm so sorry about your troubles, Lisa. Have you seen Tom yet?"

"Just got in last night. I'm hoping to see him tomorrow. The flowers are lovely, Dan."

"They're from the English flower garden that Liz planned before she died."

"Dan, I didn't know. When did this happen?"

He told her of the circumstances. It was good to have someone with whom to talk. "I'm still at loose ends. Luckily, I have an excellent nurse for the girls—a live-in nanny, as Liz called her. It all happened so suddenly. I can't seem to get back to reality. To make plans."

"If I can be of any help, Dan . . ."

He smiled. "You have troubles enough of your own, Lisa, but maybe we can cry on each other's shoulder from time to time."

Chapter Fourteen
Who Is Guilty?

Lisa greeted Kent and Banks enthusiastically the next day. They were all eager to get started with their private investigation. When Roger Daniels arrived half an hour later, they were ready to compare notes.

"I have a little more information," Roger Daniels contributed. "Michael Shea came by Tom's house and picked him up. A neighbor remembers seeing Tom get into Shea's car."

So Tom did not go to Michael Shea's office on his own. It deepened the mystery.

Once again Lisa remembered her mother's words. "Michael Shea killed Michael Shea." She toyed with the idea of telling the men about Tom's confession and how Shea had used it to blackmail both Tom and her. But Shea had burned the confession. There was no proof that it had even existed. Besides, it furnished a motive for Tom's attack. She decided not to mention it, at least until she had talked to Tom.

Michael Shea had had a number of ladies in his past. In all probability he had discarded a few along the way.

There had been the nurse at the hospital who'd left Oakdale soon after Michael had dropped her. A friend of the nurse had told Roger Daniels that another woman had been involved. A nightclub entertainer had been the rival.

Lisa had heard of the nightclub entertainer too. Kent and Banks decided to follow that slim lead. It shouldn't be too difficult—Oakdale did not have all that many nightclubs. But first they wanted to visit Michael Shea's office and go over it with the proverbial fine-tooth comb.

Roger Daniels called Memorial General and asked to speak to Dan Stewart. He explained the situation. Of course Banks and Kent could check out Shea's office. It was still unoccupied. The police had given it the once-over, but otherwise it was pretty much as he had left it. Banks and Kent left for the hospital.

After they had gone, Roger Daniels talked briefly with Lisa. "Can't you get some rest?" he asked. "You've been through such a lot."

"I must see Tom first."

After Roger left, she called Annie.

"Your mother doesn't seem so well today. Just sort of listless, you know. And weaker, definitely weaker." For once there was no voice from the other room saying, "Don't tell her stuff like that, you ninny!"

"Call the doctor," Lisa instructed Annie. "Ask him to come out. Maybe she should be taken to the hospital."

"We'll see," Annie said. "And I'll call you and tell you what the doctor says."

Lisa hung up. She was tired, desperately tired, but it was time to get ready for her visit to Tom. She wanted to see him. She must see him. And yet she dreaded the visit.

She arrived at the jail at four o'clock. Tom had returned from the court. They were still wrangling over the jury selection.

He came into the visitors' room. She'd been afraid that she'd be talking to him through a sort of wire cage, as she had seen in the movies. An officer stood just outside the open door, but they were really alone.

She hugged him. He looked so young and so forlorn, but she wouldn't let herself cry. She needed to be strong for him.

"It's good to see you, Mom."

"Tom, I've hired detectives. I'm positive they'll unearth something that will help you."

"I killed him, Mom."

She brushed his words aside, although her head ached with the weight of them. "I've told no one about the confession, Tom." She spoke in a low voice to prevent the officer from overhearing. "But could it possibly help for your lawyer and the detectives to know about it?"

"There is no confession, Mom."

"I know," she said. "Michael burned it."

"Mom, that was a copy. He told me and laughed at how stupid you had been to think he would burn the original."

"Then . . ." She didn't understand.

"He was trying to blackmail me again with the original. He wanted me to tell him where you and Chuckie had gone."

"Oh, my God!" The pain in her head was something she must ignore.

"He was taunting me, Mom, and saying awful things about you. I threw myself at him, knocked him down." He stopped for a moment as if reliving the scene. "Afterwards, I took the confession out of his hand. I burned it on the way to the police station."

The officer appeared in the doorway. "Sorry," he said. "Time's up."

"I'll be back tomorrow, Tom."

"Don't worry so, Mom." He kissed her and was gone.

She sat there for a moment, too weak to rise. So Tom had fought Michael Shea in her defense. She too was to blame for Michael's death. Had it not been for her, Tom would never have attacked the man. The pain in her head was blinding. Suddenly she toppled from the chair and fell to the floor.

It was only a matter of minutes until the officer returned and found her. She was unconscious. A police ambulance rushed her to Memorial General.

In Mexico City, Jay Watson wondered why Lisa had not called. The day had been a complicated one for her, he knew. Still he worried.

And Annie wondered why Lisa didn't answer the phone. She wanted to tell her that the doctor had said there was no cause for alarm yet. Alma Miller was bound to have several ups and downs as the disease progressed.

In Michael Shea's office, Banks and Kent were unaware that the lady who had hired them was in a coma. They had unearthed some interesting things. Nothing quite fit together, but there was always a chance that the missing piece of the puzzle might turn up. In one of Shea's desk drawers they had found a lady's earring—not valuable, but very distinctive. It was a green stone rose. Why had Michael Shea saved it? Where was the other one?

There was a discarded desk calendar that also proved interesting. A phone number appeared and reappeared. In one place there was the note "Floor show at ten." They had already obtained a list of Oakdale nightclubs. It was easy enough to identify the phone number as that of the Domino Club. Banks and Kent decided to do a little nightclubbing. It would be interesting to see what the floor show was like.

They had just finished their search of Shea's office when Dan Stewart entered. "Lisa Shea is in our hospital," he told them. "She's in a coma. We haven't determined how serious it is." As if awaiting instructions, they waited for him to continue. "One thing I'm sure of," he went on, "she would expect you to carry on with your investigation. Roger Daniels will be the person to report to now." There was a pause. "Do you have a place to stay?"

"Not yet, but we'll find one."

"Why not stay with me? I have a big house with a lot of empty rooms. A good cook, too." He smiled. "And two daughters who'll be terribly impressed to have detectives in the house." He gave them his address and directions for getting there.

"We'll be late." They told him of their plans to visit the Domino Club, and why.

"Good sleuthing!" From his key ring he slipped off an extra key. "Front door," he said. "The porch will be lit up. And I'll probably be up. I don't go to bed very early."

Dan Stewart returned to check on Lisa. She had been given a thorough examination. There was no stroke as far as anyone could tell. Her pulse was strong. Blood pressure was high, but not alarmingly so. Still she continued deep in a coma. It was as though her mind had decided to escape reality for awhile. There was nothing to do but watch and wait.

In his office, Roger Daniels had reached a decision.

There was nothing to be gained by telling Tom Hughes of his mother's condition. In time, he would have to, but not now. The boy had enough to face as it was.

Banks and Kent drove to the Domino Club, reaching there about nine-thirty. It was a busy night. A county basketball conference was on, bringing money people into the area. As games were won and lost at the Oakdale Center, spectators drifted into the Domino Club to celebrate or to complain about the referees.

The detectives found a table in a smoky corner near the stage. At that point, they did not intend to disclose their identity.

A waiter approached, and they ordered drinks. As they sipped them, they looked around. The crowd was noisy. Here and there, standing backs against the walls in the shadows, were several sinister-looking men. Bouncers perhaps. Maybe an owner or two. The Domino, they had learned, was owned by a Chicago group. It was considered one of the more successful clubs in the area.

"I think," Banks said, "that if we learn anything here, we're going to have to tell someone in charge who we are."

"Right."

They motioned to their waiter. "We'd like to see the manager or anyone who's in charge," Kent told him.

"Everything all right?" the waiter asked nervously.

"Everything's fine. Just bring us the manager."

It was several minutes before a heavy-set, swarthy character appeared at their table. He removed the cigar from his mouth. "I'm in charge here. What can I do for you?"

"Can you sit down for a minute?"

He sat.

They pulled out their identification. "No problems with the Domino," Banks assured him. "We're just here trying to get a little background information on Michael Shea."

Their man looked relieved.

"Did you happen to know him?" Kent asked.

"Doc Shea? Sure. He was a regular customer until a while back. Too bad about his being killed."

"What can you tell us about him?" It was Kent again.

The man shrugged. "Not much. He was sort of closemouthed, if you know what I mean, but dependable."

"What do you mean, dependable?" Banks asked.

"Well, you know . . . now and then there'd be a little trouble here. A fight maybe. Somebody hurt. We'd call the doc and he'd come out and fix the person up. No questions. No reporting things to the police. He'd do us a favor and we'd do favors for him."

"What kind of favors?"

"Oh, nothing big. He had his favorite table, his favorite drink. He liked the special attention. And we never charged him nothin'. That was a house rule." He gave them a knowing smile. "Had his favorite broad, too. We fixed him up with her."

Banks and Kent tried to look not too interested. "The gal? Is she still here?"

"You'll see her tonight. She's the main attraction. Lorraine Durcel. The crowd likes her, though she's not my type."

They thanked him, and he left their table.

The floor show began with the usual fanfare. Banks and Kent waited patiently for the main attraction.

Lorraine Durcel came on. If she had been told that detectives were out front asking about Michael Shea, she gave no indication. She did her routine—the innocent interpretation of the suggestive song. The performance was polished and the crowd loved it. She pouted and preened and gave them the baby stare as the songs became more risqué. And she was clever enough to leave the audience wanting more.

"Hard as rocks, that one." Kent observed after she left the stage. "I have a feeling she's been told by now that we're here. She'll be waiting for us in her dressing room."

They paid their check, with a generous tip. Banks glanced at one of the men standing against the wall. "We'd like to meet Miss Durcel." The man nodded his head affirmatively and led them backstage.

They introduced themselves to Lorraine Durcel. "We're with the Delacourt Detective Agency. No cause for alarm. We're just trying to learn a little more about Michael Shea."

"Oh, my," she said. "Real detectives, like in the movies."

"We understand you knew Dr. Shea," Banks said.

She widened her eyes, lit a cigarette, and fanned the smoke away.

Fencing for time, Banks thought, and glanced at Kent. This was a cautious babe.

"Michael Shea and I were friends. Nothing serious, just friends. I was sorry to learn that he died." Her words were cold. "But we hadn't seen him here for quite a while. After he married, he stopped showing up. Guess we weren't good enough for him."

Kent cleared his throat. "Did he ever mention Tom Hughes?"

"Oh, no. We never talked much about other people he knew. He worked hard. He just liked to come here and relax and listen to my act. Sometimes we danced.

He was a good dancer. And he thought I was great. 'Some day,' he told me, 'you're gonna be a big star in Chicago or maybe even New York.'" She stubbed out her cigarette and looked at them almost defiantly. "And I will be, too. Just like he said."

They thanked her. "We enjoyed your act, Miss Durcel, and we'll be watching for you in Chicago. We'll be leaving now."

But they didn't leave. Outside in the car they waited for the second floor show to go on. They planned a quick search of her dressing room while she was on stage.

There was no need to wait for the second floor show. No more than thirty minutes had passed when they saw her slip out the door of the Domino Club and hail a cruising cab.

In an instant they were at her side. "Not so fast, Miss Durcel," Banks told her.

"I think maybe we should continue our talk a bit," Kent said.

They walked her back inside and to her dressing room. "Now you just sit there like a good girl while we do a bit of looking around."

Kent stood by her chair. Banks went through her dressing table, drawer by drawer. At last he came to what he was looking for. "Interesting," he said. He held up the delicately carved green rose earring.

"So what?" she snapped.

"We found the other one in Michael Shea's office," Kent told her.

"And now," Banks said, "let's have a look at what you were planning to take with you."

Kent handed him Lorraine's bag.

"You can't do that," she said, grabbing for it. "You don't have a search warrant."

"You see too many movies," Banks told her. Methodically, he went through the bag. Some clothing, cosmetics, sleeping pills, and a pack of letters. In a side pocket which he almost overlooked, his fingers felt an object easily identified. He unzipped the pocket and carefully extracted, using a tissue from the bag, a small pistol. He held it up.

"I always carry that," she said. "It can be dangerous out here. It's late at night when I go home."

"Do you have a permit?" Banks asked. He was thumbing through the packet of letters. There were several addressed to Michael Shea, returned, unopened. "I think we'd better visit headquarters and get better acquainted," Banks said.

On their way out, they saw their waiter. "Tell her boss that Miss Durcel won't be appearing in any more floor shows tonight." They left for the police station.

At Memorial General Hospital, Lisa Shea had suddenly, inexplicably come out of the coma. She stared at the nurse by her bedside and smiled. "Where am I?"

"In the hospital, ma'am."

"What happened to me?"

"Now you just be quiet and I'll call the doctor."

While she lay there and waited, Lisa drowsily wondered what hospital she was in. Her mind seemed a complete blank, an unwritten diary. "It will come back," she told herself. "I'll remember." But she did feel peaceful. "Lisa Miller," she said aloud. Was that her name? It seemed not quite right. She must have been quite ill, and for some time, too.

A doctor entered the room. "Lisa," he asked, "how are you feeling?"

He looked familiar and she felt she could trust him.

"Where am I, doctor?" she asked him.

It was obvious to Dan Stewart that she did not recognize him. Memory often returned slowly after a deep coma. "You're a patient at Memorial General Hospital in Oakdale, Illinois."

The words had a familiar ring to them.

"There's nothing to worry about. You've had a shock. It's over now. I'm going to give you an injection so you can rest some more. When you wake up, I'm sure everything will be clearer."

She smiled at him. He was very kind.

"I'm Dr. Dan Stewart, your doctor. I'll be close by." As he left her room, he wondered if things would be clearer when she awakened. He must call Roger Daniels immediately. He understood that the last of the jurors would be selected in the morning and that the trial would begin immediately.

He dialed Roger Daniels's home phone. "Roger. Dan Stewart speaking. Lisa's come out of her coma. She's suffering from amnesia. I'm hoping it's temporary."

On the way to the police station, Lorraine Durcel became increasingly agitated. "I could certainly use a drink," she told the detectives. It appeared to them that possibly she'd had a couple of quick ones while they waited in their car.

"Michael Shea wasn't worth all this trouble," she said suddenly. Then she became silent and said nothing until after they reached the police station.

The police sergeant listened while they explained why they had brought her in. "We have reason to believe she's withholding important evidence pertaining to the Michael Shea case. She was also carrying this pistol without a permit. Without doubt, she should be held as a material witness." In a sense, they were trumped-up charges, but Banks and Kent were playing a hunch. The police sergeant seemed inclined to go along with them.

"I want a lawyer," Lorraine shouted. "I'm getting a raw deal here and I damn well know it. I want a lawyer." She pounded on the table.

The police sergeant said she could get a lawyer or they'd get one for her. She ignored him, lashing out instead. "I have connections in Chicago. Important connections. A word from them in the right places and you third-rate pipsqueaks could be squashed like bugs. You can't pin anything on me."

Kent regarded her with renewed interest. "Who said we were trying to pin anything on you?" he asked innocently. "We're just asking some simple questions."

Banks was reading the letters she had sent to Shea which had been returned. She made a lunge for them. "Give them to me. They're mine."

Banks told her, "These are threatening letters." He played his hunch. "After Shea returned your letters unanswered, when did you go to see him? What happened, Lorraine?"

She began to cry.

"You rest awhile, Miss," the police sergeant said.

Several hours later in the Oakdale County courthouse, the last juror was selected. Tom Hughes studied the faces of the men and women who would decide his fate. Two of the men were old enough to be his grandfather. He liked their looks. There was a small woman with a sweet, concerned face. The foreman had been selected. Tom remembered that he had been the only college graduate of the lot. There was an intense-looking young woman, no more than thirty, and a black man who had tried his best to get excused and had failed. The others were fairly nondescript.

The judge was a man apparently in his mid-fifties. He had a high brow, white hair and weary eyes. He looked as though he had been picked for the part by some Hollywood casting director. Now he was making some preliminary remarks to the jury.

Tom looked around the room. His mother was nowhere to be seen. Chris and Nancy Hughes were there. He nodded to them and they smiled reassuringly. Leaning towards Roger Daniels, he whispered, "Mom isn't here. Is anything the matter?"

Roger was casual. "That investigation, perhaps. Don't worry." He didn't like evading the truth but certainly until they knew if Lisa's amnesia was temporary, Tom should be told nothing.

The judge cleared his throat. "Court is recessed until tomorrow."

It was almost noon when Lisa awakened from the sedation that Dan Stewart had given her. This time the hospital bed was no surprise. She remembered the nurse and the kind doctor. This was Memorial General Hospital and the doctor . . . she willed the vision of him back into her memory. Dan Stewart, of course. But what was Lisa Miller—no, no—Lisa Shea doing in Memorial General Hospital? She would have to concentrate on that. She rang for the nurse. "I'm better," she told the pleasant-looking woman. "And quite thirsty. Could I have some water?"

The nurse obliged. "We'll have a tray here for you soon—a sort of brunch." She busied herself about the room.

Everything seemed confusing to Lisa. She was still trying to piece things together when Dan Stewart entered the room. "Lisa, you're better. I can tell." He checked the chart at the foot of the bed.

"I'm so mixed-up, Dan. Is Michael dead?"

He nodded. "But don't try too hard to remember everything at once. It will all come back gradually. The thing now is to get well. At the rate you're improving, you should be released soon."

Suddenly two names popped into her mind. Jay Watson and Roger Daniels. "Can I talk to Roger Daniels?" she asked. "I want him to call a friend for me in . . . in Mexico City."

"I'll do better than that," said Dan Stewart. "I'll call Roger and ask him to come by."

He started to leave. "Dan?" She reached for his hand. Her eyes looked at him pleadingly.

"Did I kill Michael Shea? You can tell me. I must know."

"Absolutely not, Lisa. Erase that thought from your mind."

"I could have, you know," she said softly. "I could have."

"Lisa, you were on your way to Mexico when he died."

"Running away," she said, "as usual." Slowly it was all coming back to her.

"Try to get some more sleep, Lisa." He pointed out some medication to the nurse. "A couple of these should help her have a little nap."

When Roger Daniels arrived, she had had her "little nap" and was feeling refreshed and stronger.

"Roger, I want you to call Jay Watson. You have his number, don't you?"

He nodded.

"Tell him I sort of blacked out, but I'm much better now, and I'll be calling him soon."

"I'll explain, Lisa," Roger promised.

"And Chuckie." She remembered now. The little pony. Chuckie's fall and broken leg. The trip back to the house and to the doctor. "Ask him how Chuckie is."

"I will, Lisa."

After he left, she sat up on the side of the bed. There was someplace she must go. Something she must do. She fought to remember.

There had been a new and astounding development in Lorraine Durcel's involvement with Michael Shea. Kent and Banks had been working around the clock. They had checked on all the personnel they could find who had been on duty the morning of Michael Shea's death. They questioned a Miss Tweedy, a receptionist, who was at the main desk.

"It was a quiet morning," she said. "I remember it so well because of the awful thing that happened to Dr. Shea."

"Would you have seen anyone headed for Dr. Shea's office?" Kent asked.

"Not necessarily," she said. "Most people do come by my desk, though." She remembered when Dr. Shea came in with the young man. "You would never have guessed what was about to happen."

Banks produced a picture of Lorraine Durcel. "By any chance did you see this lady that morning?"

She studied the picture carefully, holding it up to the light. "Yes," she answered firmly. "Of course. She stopped at my desk and asked how to get to Dr. Shea's office. I thought nothing of it at the time. As far as I knew, he was still there with the young man."

Banks held the picture in front of her. "You would identify this in court as a photo of the young lady who stopped by your desk and inquired about the way to Dr. Shea's office?"

"Yes, sir."

"Thank you very much. You've been most helpful." They hurried to the police station.

The police sergeant who had been so cooperative before was once again on duty. They had the feeling he must live there. Banks told him of the positive identification that Mrs. Tweedy had made. It was imperative that they question Lorraine Durcel again. The sergeant dispatched a policeman to bring her in.

It was over quickly.

Desperate people, guilty people, can only brazen it out to a point where the evidence piles up against them. Lorraine's court-appointed lawyer hadn't been able to prepare her for that. They confronted Lorraine with the evidence. It was now known that she had gone to Michael Shea's office on that fateful morning. Banks added a guess of his own. "You arrived there after he'd had the fight with Tom."

"I didn't know what had happened. I only knew that he was there on the floor. I thought he was dead." She started crying. "I was glad that he was dead. He had told me he would never see me again." Her tear-stained face implored them to understand. "I bent over him. I had come there to kill him and someone had beat me to it. While I stared at his bloodied face, he moved. His eyelids fluttered. He was not dead." She was breathing heavily and stopped to gain control, but she seemed unable to stop talking. "I'd brought the pistol with me that you found. I shot him behind the ear." She sobbed convulsively. "I'm the one who killed Michael Shea, not that kid they have on trial!"

Banks and Kent left the station quickly. There was no time to waste. Permission was needed immediately to exhume the body of Michael Shea—the man who had been buried as the victim of a fatal beating . . . though a confessed killer now claimed to have shot him.

Chapter Fifteen
Final Curtain

Lisa could hardly wait for Dan Stewart's visit to her hospital room. Her memory was back. Fuzzy around the edges at points, but the main pieces were in place. Tom was unjustly accused of murder. She had detectives working on an investigation. Maybe they would unearth some facts which would help Tom's case. Had the trial started yet?

Dan Stewart entered her room. "I'm ready to be released, Dan. I've recovered my senses." She gave him a memory recital.

"Very good, Lisa. You've come a long way very quickly. I'm proud of you."

"Dan, has the trial begun?"

"Just started, Lisa. Yesterday they established things like time and place and circumstances. Today will be more of the same. A few witnesses called. Tomorrow things will really get under way."

"I plan to be there tomorrow, Dan."

"I'll be there with you, Lisa. Just in case my patient needs a cough drop."

Roger Daniels was in the courtroom, but he sent an assistant to pick up Lisa at the hospital and drive her home. Polly Ashton was young, bright, eager, competent, and helpful. "I have instructions," she told Lisa. "I'm to stay with you the rest of the day and tonight and drive you to the court. I hope you don't mind. I'm very handy. I can shop, and cook too."

"I'm very grateful," Lisa said.

They reached the house. Polly was a paralegal working in Roger Daniels' office and she loved working for him. Lisa surmised that the girl was a bit starry-eyed about him. She didn't blame her. Roger had been a godsend, or more accurately, a Chris-and-Nancy-Hughes-send. She must thank them when she could.

Polly unloaded the car. They prepared a shopping list, and Polly set out for the nearby mall. It was too early to call Jay Watson, but perhaps she could contact Banks and Kent. When Polly returned, Lisa asked if she knew how to get in touch with the two men. Polly whipped out a little black book and Lisa called the number. A pleasant voice answered. The gentlemen were out and not expected back for some time. Later tonight they might be reached at this number. Obviously, they were staying at Dan Stewart's. One more good deed that he had done.

"You lie down and rest," Polly told her. "I'll prepare a bite to eat."

Later Lisa called Jay and assured him she felt better herself and somehow better about Tom. "Chuckie's fine. Mending fast," Jay told her. She sighed with relief and joined Polly in the kitchen to see if she could help.

Lisa didn't know it, but at that moment, Banks and Kent were in the Oakdale cemetery. They had received permission to exhume the body of Michael Shea. Dr.

Ragsdale, fortunately, was away, but an assistant from the coroner's office would accompany them to the morgue for further examination on the body. It was a grisly business!

They found a small-caliber bullet hole behind Michael Shea's ear, as Lorraine had said. An autopsy confirmed without doubt that death had been caused by the bullet which had penetrated the brain. The bullet was recovered. It had come from the small pistol that Lorraine Durcel had carried.

They worked until very late, tried repeatedly to call Roger Daniels but failed to reach him. He would appear in court tomorrow unaware of the new evidence.

Dan Stewart was still up when they let themselves in around midnight. He heard their story. They cautioned him against mentioning it to anyone before it was presented to the judge and the lawyers. Dan told them that he'd be with Lisa in court. In case the new revelation was too much of a shock for her, he'd have a tranquilizer ready. They said good night and stumbled to bed.

As Polly and Lisa drove to court the following morning, Polly said, "Here's something Roger Daniels said to warn you about. I didn't want to bother you with it yesterday."

Fear clutched Lisa's heart. What now?

Polly continued. "Michael Shea's mother will be in the courtroom. She came up from Memphis for the memorial service and has been staying with friends in Chicago."

All Lisa could manage was an "Oh!"

They reached the courthouse. Dan Stewart was there, smiling, waiting for her. "How do you feel, Lisa?"

She looked him straight in the eye. "Up to it."

"Good girl," he responded.

They walked into the courthouse. The courtroom was jammed. Lisa spotted Marvel Shea immediately. She was dressed in black. There was something about her that reminded Lisa of Michael. It was apparent that she had once been a beautiful woman. Occasionally, she dabbed at her eyes with a lacy black handkerchief. She was completely the grief-stricken mother. Lisa felt the urge to applaud.

Someone whispered something to Marvel Shea and she turned to look at Lisa. For an awful moment, Lisa feared that the woman was going to leave her seat and come over to speak with her. It would be a showy, attention-getting thing to do.

But suddenly there was action in the courtroom. The judge entered and everyone stood. Court was in session.

Tom sat just ahead of Lisa with Roger Daniels at his side. He seems to look younger all the time, Lisa thought, and fought back tears.

Dr. Shea's nurse was the first witness called. Yes, she recognized Tom Hughes. He had been in the office several times after the car accident. Yes, it was true. Twice she had heard loud voices behind the closed door. It was the boy who was shouting. He seemed quite angry, though she didn't know how anyone could be angry at a fine man like Dr. Shea. The last statement was stricken from the record, but not stricken from the jurors' memories, Lisa thought.

A number of Memorial Hospital staff people were called, all testifying to Michael Shea's ability as a doctor. With each statement as to his excellence, Marvel Shea turned and shot a triumphant look at Lisa. She wiped her eyes with her fluff of a handkerchief. Smudge-proof eye make-up. Lisa noted.

It was almost noon when there was a commotion at the back of the courtroom. Banks and Kent, portfolios bulging, were led by a deputy up to the judge's bench. There was an extended conference. The courtroom buzzed. The judge rapped his gavel. "I'd like to confer with the lawyers in my chambers. Court is adjourned until two-thirty." He rose and disappeared, his black robe flapping, as they all got to their feet.

Lisa managed to catch Tom's eye as they led him out. She gave him the most encouraging smile that she could manage.

At lunch with Dan and Polly, she asked them, "Whatever do you think that was all about?"

Dan smiled. "It looks like new evidence, doesn't it? Let's hope and pray." He said no more.

They were reconvened by two-thirty. Still no judge. Still no lawyers. Even the jury had not been called back in. The spectators, with nothing to look at, grew restless. It was inevitable that Marvel Shea would flutter to Lisa's side. "Mrs. Shea, Ah'm Michael's mother." She blew her nose daintily. "Such a tragedy for all of us."

"You must call me Lisa." It was all she could think of to say.

"And how is mah grandson Chuckie? Ah do hope he becomes a 'Charles' when he's older. Such an elegant name—Charles."

Lisa smiled. "Perhaps while you're here, you can come by the house. Wouldn't you like something of Michael's as a memento?"

"Oh, my deah. Ah'm ovahcome. Absolutely ovahcome." She pressed the ever-present handkerchief to her eyes.

There was a stir in the courtroom. The jury was

filing in. "We'll get together," Lisa assured her and smiled wanly.

Marvel Shea scurried back to her seat. The lawyers filed in and Tom took his place. Roger Daniels looked at Lisa and at Chris and Nancy Hughes. His eyes were bright, but his face was carefully composed.

The entry call was sounded for the judge. The spectators stood. Lisa looked at the courtroom clock. It was exactly three-forty-three.

The judge summoned the lawyers. Tom was instructed to stand. "Due to new evidence now disclosed, this case is dismissed, as is the jury. A new trial based on the evidence just presented to this court will be scheduled in the near future. I have instructed that the defendant, Thomas Miller Hughes, is to be freed on bail and will confer with him and his lawyer in my chambers. Case dismissed."

Dan Stewart gripped Lisa's arm. "Are you all right?"

Her cheeks were flushed. Her eyes were shining. "I never felt better." She threw Tom a kiss as he left the courtroom with Roger Daniels.

Marvel Shea was at her side. "You could have knocked me ovah with a feather," she said. "It was jest lak in the movies, wasn't it?" She looked at Lisa directly. This time there was no pretense in her eyes. "Ah'm very happy for your son, mah deah."

"Where are you staying, Mrs. Shea?"

"Please call me Marvel. Ah'd lak for you to call me Marvel."

"Where are you staying, Marvel?"

"At the Oakridge Motel."

"I'll call you tonight. Perhaps you can come by tomorrow."

"Mah friends in Chicago are comin' down heah to get me tomorrow. They could bring me by. Ah'd like for them to meet you," Marvel added with a smile.

Friends crowded around Lisa congratulating her. Far in the back she saw Kent and Banks. "See you at the house in an hour or so," she called. "We must celebrate."

She asked Dan to join them, but he begged off. "I'm sure work has piled up at the hospital." He kissed her. "I'm very, very happy for you, Lisa Shea."

Polly drove her home but wouldn't come in. "Roger will have a lot of work for me to do," she said. "He'll be needing me." She was excited and happy.

Once in the house, Lisa made two telephone calls. The first was to Annie. "How's Mom?"

"Pretty spry today," Annie answered.

She told Annie the good news and heard her repeating it to Alma Miller. Her mother's voice came through clear and strong. "I knew it all along. Get the particulars, you ninny!"

"Tell Mom I'll be out and explain everything. Tomorrow or the next day for sure."

She got through to Jay. "I'll know more later, darling, but they've dismissed the case against Tom and are scheduling a new trial."

He congratulated her. "I love you. I miss you."

"Maybe when the Colemans bring Chuckie home, you can come along and get acquainted with Oakdale."

He promised.

The party was not a hilarious one. The occasion was too momentous for that. Banks and Kent told her step by step what they had discovered and how Lorraine Durcel had eventually confessed. Poor Lorraine, she thought, another victim of Michael's.

The doorbell rang. It was Nancy and Chris Hughes. "We just dropped by to share our happiness with you,"

Nancy said, hugging Lisa warmly.

It was almost an hour later when Tom walked in with Roger Daniels. They toasted both of them, the boy and his lawyer, and then they toasted the two detectives from Chicago who had made this occasion possible.

The house seemed to glow with happiness. "My cup runneth over," Lisa said as someone filled her champagne glass. She too was glowing with happiness.

As promised, Lisa called Marvel Shea. She and her friends from Chicago arrived by ten o'clock the next morning. Lisa had coffee and rolls waiting.

"Mah goodness, what a lovely house," Marvel exclaimed. "Was it yours or Michael's?"

Lisa ignored the question. She had found several things of Michael's that she thought Marvel might like to have—a class ring, his medical diploma, a handsome wristwatch. Marvel took them all.

As they prepared to leave, she drew Lisa aside. "Was there a will, mah dear?"

"I honestly don't know. I'm sure the lawyers will be in touch."

"Ah hope there was a little somethin' foah me," she said wistfully. "It would be helpful. Yes, it would."

Lisa watched the small woman march down the walk to the waiting car. She looked fragile, but she had strength and perseverance. She would survive.

It was four months later. The second trial was over. Tom was completely exonerated and although Lorraine had been found guilty, the sentence had not been a heavy one.

Lisa and Tom were having a quiet supper for two and discussing their future. Tom had decided to go back to school. He wanted to become a lawyer. Both

Lisa and Bob Hughes would help him with his schooling.

"And what about you, Mom?"

She wasn't sure. The Colemans had brought a good-as-new-Chuckie back, but Jay Watson had not returned with them. Absence, it seemed, had not made the heart grow fonder.

Someone was at the door. Dan Stewart was standing there. He had dropped by to say goodbye. Oakdale haunted him with too many unhappy memories. Bob Hughes had obtained an excellent appointment for him at a London hospital. He was taking Emily and Betsy with him. "An old world—a new life," he said to Lisa.

She would miss him.

"There's one thing more," he told her. "Would you be interested in becoming the manager of Wade's Bookstore?"

She promised to consider it. She had often thought that the world of business was fascinating. After urging her to take the job, Dan left.

Tom had studying to do, so he said good night.

Lisa sat alone before the early fall fire and stared into the flames as though they might foretell the future. She and Tom were closer than ever before. Things seemed to be back to normal. She was eager to get on with tomorrow. . . .

You can now order previous titles of *Soaps & Serials*™ Books by mail!

Just complete the order form, detach, and send together with your check or money order payable to:

Soaps & Serials™
120 Brighton Road, Box 5201
Clifton, NJ 07015-5201

- - - - - - - - - - - - - - - - - - - -

Please <u>circle</u> the book #'s you wish to order:

The Young and The Restless	1	2	3	4
Days of Our Lives	1	2	3	4
Guiding Light	1	2	3	4
Another World	1	2	3	4
As The World Turns	1	2	3	4
Capitol™	1	2	3	4
Dallas™	1	2	3	4
Knots Landing™	1	2	3	4

Each book is $2.50 ($3.25 in Canada).

Total number of books circled _____ × price above = $ _____ .

Sales tax (CT residents only) $ _____ .

Shipping and Handling $ _____ .95

Total payment enclosed $ _____ .
(check or money orders only)

Name _____

Address _____ Apt# _____

City _____

State _____ Zip _____

Telephone (_____) _____

Area code   ATWT 4

Soaps & Serials™ Fans!

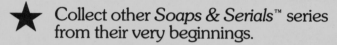

★ Order the *Soaps & Serials*™ books you have missed in this series.

★ Collect other *Soaps & Serials*™ series from their very beginnings.

★ Give *Soaps & Serials*™ series as gifts to other fans.

...see other side for ordering information